The Scots and the
Sassenachs

THE DUKE'S LOST LOVE

RAVEN MCALLAN &
CASSIE O'BRIEN

The Duke's Lost Love
ISBN # 978-1-80250-527-6
©Copyright Raven McAllan & Cassie O'Brien 2023
Cover Art by Erin Dameron-Hill ©Copyright February 2023
Interior text design by Claire Siemaszkiewicz
Totally Bound Publishing

Totally Bound Publishing books by Cassie O'Brien

Single Books
The Girls' Club
From a Lady to a Maid
Ellie's Rules

THE DUKE'S
LOST LOVE

Dedication

To Wendy, the best cheerleader ever,
and to the two Pauls,
for putting up with our ramblings.

Chapter One

Now

By the light of a flaming flambeau held aloft by
Sydney, page and general dogsbody to the Armstrong
household, Mrs Evanna Percival-Smyth walked home.
The moon was on the wane and that, added to the
heavy cloud obscuring the stars in the night sky, made
his illuminating assistance to guide her footsteps a
necessity. A trip, with its likely consequence of a
twisted ankle, was high on the cards otherwise.

Her house was cloaked in near darkness when she
arrived. No servant would be up waiting. She was not
meant to be there, but rather at Denny House, where
she'd accepted an appointment to chaperone the Lady
Cairstine McColl during her visit to Corbridge.

Circumstances had led to this unexpected return.

Of course, if she chose, she could wake the
household and have people ready to do her bidding
immediately—or almost immediately. It would mean
they would have to dress and hurry, probably bleary-

eyed or yawning, from their various rooms, and Evanna was more considerate than to ask for that. She valued her staff. Why should her unforeseen homecoming disturb their slumber? In her mind they got little enough respite as it was.

Plus, she had a lot to think about and didn't want anyone to see her agitation. Sydney, bless him, did not count. His intelligence was not of the highest, but he was always willing to please.

At her front door, she opened her reticule and passed her young escort a silver sixpence. His eyes widened.

"Cor, Mrs P. Thank you."

She patted his shoulder and smiled, even though, with her knees all a tremble after seeing Cairstine's father, Nathan, for the first time in over twenty years, it was the last thing she felt like doing. She wanted to run and hide. Be alone.

Think things over.

Sydney stared at her, a slight frown creasing the space between his eyebrows. "You all right, Mrs P? You looked a bit strange just then."

Bless him. "You're a good lad, Sydney. I'm fine, just tired I suspect. Run along now. I imagine there will be plenty for you to do tomorrow. Is your bed ready?"

He nodded. "Course it is. I's been mekking it tidy every morning like what you told me to."

"Good boy. Take the flambeau to guide you but be sure to extinguish it in the water bucket when you get home."

He nodded and dashed off.

Evanna watched him disappear and reached into her reticule, which along with a quantity of small change also contained her door key. She let herself in and sighed in satisfaction at the familiar scent of her own home—lavender and beeswax. Her housemaid had obviously not skimped on either the elbow grease or the furniture polish while she'd been away. An oil lamp, its wick turned down low, lit the interior and saved her fumbling about in the dark. It took but a second to pluck it from a small consul table and make her way up the stairs to her boudoir. By the lamp's absence her servants would know she had returned.

Her thoughts were all over the place as she considered the events of the evening just gone. A large sherry to calm her agitation was in order, she decided. Once it was poured, Evanna settled back into her chair and thought back to when it had all started. Her first and only visit to Edinburgh…

* * * *

Before

The excitement began when she overheard her father's dour tones followed by her mother's firm but snappish retort from the other side of a not-quite-closed door.

"It would cost a small fortune. I'm nae made o' money for you to fritter away on female foibles and frolicking, woman."

"It's got nothing to do with frolicking or frittering, Angus Kerr," her mama retorted with a hard edge to her voice that Evanna had never heard her employ when addressing Papa before. Forceful. That was it. Intrigued, she continued to listen.

"Evanna is the prettiest of our girls as well as the eldest. Just give me five hundred pounds to take her to Edinburgh…"

Evanna held her breath, hardly daring to hope.

9

"And I'll practically guarantee she'll catch herself a well-to-do husband. Then she can sponsor each of her younger sisters when they are of marriageable age. That's four for the price of one. Consider it an investment. After all, it's not much more than you spent on that gelding last month."

Her father fired back, "At least the gelding crossed the finishing line first and brought home the prize fund."

"An aberration no doubt." Her mother sounded less than impressed. "Let's face it, it's about time one of your stable achieved a positive result. Your racehorses cost more than all of we females do put together. The gelding's winnings should meet the majority of the expenses I'll incur in Edinburgh."

"But...but...five hundred pounds," her father said glumly. "Would fifty nae do?"

"It would not, now wheesht or I'll be demanding a thousand. You think on my words, Angus. You fathered them and you have a responsibility to see your daughters respectably established."

The rustling of stiffened petticoats warned Evanna it was time to move. She picked up her skirts and hurried away.

* * * *

Now

Nathaniel, Duke of Glenard sank gratefully into the padded comfort of a fireside chair and accepted the balloon glass of brandy offered to him by his daughter, Cairstine. The concern in her eyes mirrored the tone of her voice as he took his first sip. "You look quite knocked up, Papa. Drink this and we'll talk in the morning. There's no rush now the letter has been destroyed."

Knocked up, knocked sideways and thoroughly knocked off kilter. Nathan could only manage a nod. One image filled his mind to the exclusion of all else. There was no room for more.

Evanna… My love…

Cairstine smiled softly and walked to the door. If she was disappointed at his lack of response in not enquiring as to her own part in the affair of the treasonable letter that had brought them all hotfoot to Corbridge, she didn't show it. He would make it up to her in the morning. Ask all manner of questions about her adventures over the last few weeks. Tell of his own and express his happiness at her marrying the very man he would have chosen for her if she had not already done so herself — Duncan, the Earl of Callander. But for tonight he needed some time alone with his thoughts.

Evanna…

* * * *

Before

He had first seen her at an evening entertainment he'd attended at the Assembly Rooms in Edinburgh when his own father, Neil, had still been alive and he himself had borne the lesser title of Viscount Nathaniel McColl. His father had decided his twenty-year-old heir required a little town polish before his introduction to the height of the ton during the official London Season the following year, so had dispatched him to the Scottish capital to reside with his godfather, Sir Douglas Wallace, and experience the festivities enjoyed by the minor nobility and wealthy gentry who resided in the city. Sir Douglas' own son, Alain, was not so far above Nathan in age as for them to have little in common. Their friendship had been cemented one evening while downing an after-dinner bottle of port.

Alain winked when the dining room door swung shut behind Sir Douglas. His wife, Alain's mother, had long since retired to bed. "I fancy another round. How about you?"

Nathan, enjoying the mellow feeling imbibing the wine induced, agreed. A fresh bottle was soon delivered by way of the butler, and once it was uncorked, Alain dismissed the servant with a lazy wave of his hand. "We'll see ourselves up, thank you."

Nathan sipped and found the flavour as richly satisfying as he had the contents of the previous bottle.

"So…" Alain said. "How did you find the ladies sauntering in the park this afternoon? Did any of them catch you eye? I thought Lady Merrythorpe was looking rather hopefully in your direction. She's recently *enceinte* and free to follow her own inclinations for the next couple of months, you know?"

Nathan cheeks heated to his hesitant reply. "Ah…she is…? Um…?"

Alain hooted with laughter. "You never have, have you? Come along. Admit it. You're still as pure as the driven snow."

Nathan fidgeted uncomfortably in his seat at the truth of that particular statement. An edition of engraved prints that included Ruben's famous nudes of Venus, Angelica and Andromeda were his sole education on how men differed from women beneath their clothes. Apart from one stolen kiss under the mistletoe the previous Christmas, the book, his imagination and a fleeting glimpse of a breast when one fair matron's neckline had slipped were indeed his total experience of the fairer sex to date. "Well...not exactly."

Alain eyed him knowingly. "So, what did you get? A kiss or two? Or maybe she let you slip your hand down her bodice and feel her breast?"

That the kiss had been the extent of it, Nathan chose not to admit, so instead he nodded.

Alain grinned. "Well, that's a situation we must rectify as soon as may be. A young matron up for some fun times will at the very least expect you to know what goes where and when. Gird your loins, my friend. You and I are going pay a call at Mistress MacDonald's fine establishment tomorrow evening."

Nathan swallowed hard as nerves and mounting excitement at the prospect played their part. "We are?"

Alain tossed down the remaining port in his glass. "Be careful how much wine you take with dinner. The proprietress of the house we shall visit after it will not permit admittance to any gentleman she suspects of being too tipsy to treat her valuable merchandise with care."

Nathan set his unfinished wine down on the table and drank no more before they retired to bed. If he was to further his education with regards to the fairer sex, he'd best be on fine form come the morrow.

* * * *

It took two whole days fidgeting with tense expectation every time her mother entered the room before an announcement was finally made. The family was indeed decamping to Edinburgh for a visit to last several weeks.

Evanna was sat reading while her younger twin sisters concentrated on setting stitches into their samplers in one of the least gloomy rooms in Kerr Castle designated by their mother as the 'ladies parlour' — although the term parlour did rather flatter what had previously been a guardhouse in which the tall, open arrow slits had been glazed. Her mother entered the room and clapped her hands to garner their attention. "Girls. Your father and I have come to a decision. A house has been rented. We are removing to the capital next week."

Evanna closed her book, her tummy full of excitable wriggling worms, while her sisters sat straighter and with their eyes shining, exclaimed, "Oh, Mama. We are? How wonderful!"

Lady Kerr regarded their faces wreathed in smiles and frowned. "We are, and I expect you twins to be of use to Evanna when necessary. To walk in the park with her or accompany her on any other daytime activity where it would be unseemly for your sister to be alone. I myself will chaperone her to any evening parties, of course."

Evanna's stomach lurched guiltily as her sisters' smiles faded.

"We are not to attend the evening parties?" The twins chimed in.

"We are to be left behind?"

"That's not fair…"

"Fair has nothing to do with it," Lady Kerr stated firmly. "Evanna is the eldest and you younger girls must wait your turns. If she does well and makes a good match, she will be in a position to aid all of you when you make your own debuts but for her to do so, you two middle girls need to play your part now."

"What about me?" Robina pouted.

Lady Kerr eyed Evanna's youngest sister beadily. "Hmm… You, I will decide upon later."

Oh, goodness! I don't much like the sound of that. What happens if I don't find a suitable husband?

Evanna smiled nervously at her siblings and promised, "I will do my best."

"Of course you will," her mama said briskly. "Now, come with me. Our budget is not endless and Great Grandma's trunk awaits. Given the fuller skirts she wore, I can think of at least two dresses that when unpicked will supply enough material to fashion an evening cape and a shawl. You younger girls can have the stitching of them while Evanna reads out loud."

At this pronouncement Evanna felt ten times worse. Not only were her sisters to be denied the pleasures of music and dancing but to rub salt into the wound, as her own skill with a needle was abysmal, they had the tedious job of sewing garments they would not wear for parties they would not attend. She would make it up to them, she decided. Do her best to attract attention of a suitable beau who would be rich and handsome and good-natured enough to welcome his wife's siblings whensoever they chose to visit.

He will have to, for I will accept nothing less.

* * * *

Nathan found he could barely concentrate on his dinner with thoughts of what was to come after. It was with relief he set his glass on the table when Alain stood and excused them both to his father after only one circuit of the port bottle.

If he had tried to drink any more it would probably have choked him. Nerves were uppermost as he dwelt on what was to come. What if he couldn't perform?

Was laughed at? Gossiped about? It was not a scenario to be borne.

Common sense told him also it was not likely to happen. As Alain had explained earlier, the ladies knew what to do and enjoyed showing a virgin how to go about things.

There would not be any problems. He would, as they said, get it up, get it in and get on with it.

The evening was remarkably fine with a full moon to light their way as they walked along Canongate. Alain paused before a house that looked no different from its tall, grey residential neighbours, then pulled a black velvet opera mask from his pocket and handed it to Nathan. "You may remove it when you are private with your choice of female if you wish, but within the public room, guests remain discreetly masked."

Nathan's hand shook a little as he tied the strings at the back of his head and smoothed the soft material over his nose and the centre of his face. Using his ebony walking cane, Alain rapped on the door. Three sharp taps followed by a gap of a few seconds, then two more. It swung open and a livered footman bowed them into a lavishly decorated vestibule stylised in a theme of an Ancient Greek or Roman temple. Colonnaded stone pillars supported a vaulted ceiling and, on the walls in between them, beautifully embroidered tapestries depicted the naked frolicking of gods and goddesses that normally filled Nathan's wet dreams. A stone altar fulfilled the role of a desk and behind it, beautifully coiffured and gowned, sat a woman in her middle years.

She looked up as they entered and smiled. "Good evening, gentlemen, and welcome. You have pre-purchased invitations?"

Alain produced two gilt-edged cards with a flourish and handed them over. "Of course, Mistress MacDonald."

She surveyed them with satisfaction. "Our gold service, I see. Very good. Please proceed to the inner sanctum and enjoy all the delights our temple of love has to offer."

Nathan followed Alain through the door she indicated and tried not to gape at the females scantily clad in near translucent white Grecian robes lounging on various sofas ranged around the salon. Some were in the company of a gentleman, like himself and Alain, masked, while others sat alone and looked up with languid interest at the new arrivals. As was the vestibule, the room was lit by glass-shaded lanterns burning sweet-smelling oil and a far older lady, more modestly clothed, added to the ambiance by way of producing tinkling notes from a pianoforte.

One couple rose from a chaise, the gentleman displaying a visibly enlarged bulge at the front of his breeches. His female companion took his hand and led him from the room. A servant approached with filled wine glasses set on a silver tray. Nathan waited to follow Alain's lead as to whether he should accept one.

Alain did so and, once Nathan had taken his own, Alain told him in a low undertone, "Mistress MacDonald believes a glass or two enhances the experience, but those who wish to imbibe more would be better entertained in a drinking-den rather than her salon. Come. Let's take a casual amble around the room and find a goddess that tickles your fancy."

Nathan swallowed hard and tried not to stare at the quantity of exposed flesh on offer. Alain reassured him, "You will find no false pretence here as to the purpose of this house. It is perfectly acceptable to direct your gaze toward the feminine attributes that attract you. No person in this room is unwilling or bashful. It's the secret of Mistress MacDonald's success. The goddesses take enjoyment in the manner in which they earn their bread."

Feeling more relaxed with this knowledge, Nathan looked around him with interest and found his eyes drawn to the voluptuous curves of a raven-haired female. Excitement shivered down his spine. Her breasts were mouth wateringly luscious. They could be in his hands shortly should he wish, and his groin was telling him he very much did. He nudged Alain's arm and indicated his preference.

Alain nodded sagely. "The goddess Celeste. A good choice. I've lain with her several times. She's an experienced lover who certainly knows how to please a man. I'll walk over with you. Personally, I'm hoping the naughty little minx known as Luna is in the temple tonight. She emptied my balls three times the last time I visited."

Three times? Oh, yes please…

That his entrance ticket allowed for more than just one encounter was thrilling, and Nathan walked forward with a spring in his step. Alain bowed when they reached the lady in question. "Good evening, Celeste. May I introduce my *young* friend? Lord N is desirous of spending some time in your company?"

With a soft smile, Celeste nodded, and Nathan sensed a coded message had been sent and understood. She patted the cushioned seat beside her. "A delightful honour. Come sit beside me, my lord. Let us sit and share a glass of wine while we confide our desires."

Nathan did so and Alain walked away. Celeste beckoned a servant and once each of them had taken a freshly filled glass she looked into his eyes. "I believe you are nervous, my lord. Will you confess it? Have I the privilege of being your first coupling?"

Nathan nodded dumbly. She leant forward, took his glass, and set it down. Her breasts brushed against his chest. "I believe you would like to be private with me rather than dally in this salon?"

"Yes…"

She held out her hand. "Then our bed of pleasure awaits."

Celeste led him through an arch then up the stairs and into a corridor that had a series of closed doors along its length. A lit lantern stood on the floor outside some, but not all. She picked one up, opened the door and preceded him in. "The light signals the room is unoccupied and prepared for our use."

Nathan surveyed the room's contents, which at first glance resembled those of a boudoir, but on closer inspection contained items more unusual to find in a bedchamber than the draped bed standing at its centre. A sturdy padded stool, higher than looked comfortable to sit or perch upon, had turned wood finials jutting out at right angles on its legs. On top of the washstand glass bottles contained an oily liquid, and beside them were what appeared to be wickless candles, phallic in shape, along with a housemaid's feather duster and a pair of velvet mittens.

He began to imagine the ways in which these items could be employed, but not for long. Celeste, with a knowing half-smile, unclasped the golden belt at her waist. The silky, diaphanous material of her robe slithered from her shoulders and pooled on the floor at her feet.

Nathan stared. He couldn't help it. A still life, no matter how artfully painted, could not portray the soft, sumptuous curves of nakedness now displayed to his gaze. His hands ached to touch, and his balls tightened, demanding release.

With a sway of her hips, Celeste walked to the bed and lay down on it. "Would you care to disrobe and join me, my lord?"

Never before had Nathan shed his clothing at such a pace. Without a care for creases, his garments were soon in a heap on the floor, his bashfulness vanishing as desire to spill his seed inside this goddess increased. His manhood sprang to attention, and Celeste encouraged him to come closer while stroking her fingers between her legs.

"That's it, my lord. See, my secret place is ready and awaiting your pleasure…"

Nathan needed no second urging. Celeste parted her legs as he lay over her and guided his pre-cum-coated cock to where it most wanted to be. The sensation was beyond anything his wet dreams had provided. Warm, smooth and all-encompassing feminine softness surrounded his shaft. He let out a small moan. She lifted her hips to his and he thrust back and forth inside her — one, twice, three times — then his climax exploded. With a groan he stilled and mumbled softly. "Ah…sorry. I — "

She shushed him and kissed his neck. "There now. For a first time I would have been more surprised if it wasn't so. But you're a young man. The urge will be back with you before many minutes have passed, then we can make love again in a more leisurely manner."

Less than half an hour later, Nathan was delighted to find her words came true. The intervening time was spent exploring Celeste's naked curves as she instructed him which touches enhanced her pleasure. He learnt where her sensitive nub was hidden, how to fondle it tenderly while her excitement, and his, built.

When he mounted her once more, he was more aware of the lover beneath him and could match his thrusts to her urging rather than being wrapped up in only his own. His second climax arrived with a shout of ecstasy, and as Celeste mewled beneath him her ragged breathing gave him the hope that he had satisfied her too.

He disengaged and moved to one side. She turned toward him and held him close. He didn't mean to, but secure in her arms with his cheek resting on one plump breast and his hand cupping the other, he fell into a blissful sleep. It was daylight when he awoke. Celeste patted his bare buttock.

"Up with you, my lord. All guests must depart come the dawn."

Nathan smiled a little sheepishly. "Thank you. It was a wonderful night."

Celeste stood, picked up her robe and blew him a kiss. "Then come and see us again soon."

"You can be sure I will," he murmured as she left the room.

He re-dressed and found Alain waiting for him when he entered the vestibule. Alain winked. "There you are. About time. I don't know about you, but all this activity has left me ravenous for breakfast."

Nathan agreed, but the temple held one more surprise for him as they departed when a masked lady wearing an evening dress of the finest quality entered the vestibule from the direction of the private rooms in the company of a masked gentleman. He nudged Alain's arm. He looked, shrugged and said in an undertone, "If a couple, not wed to each other, require a little discreet privacy in which to conduct their affair, they may purchase a silver boudoir ticket from Madam.

As such, ladies are welcome here, so long as they stay within the boundaries of the rules like the gentlemen."

Nathan tried for an air of nonchalance at this unexpected turn of events. "Ah, well, yes. I suppose so."

Lord, I've got a lot to learn. I've got to come back as soon as I can. Tonight? Hmm…yes… Tonight for sure.

He found himself distracted for the rest of the day — his thoughts consumed by the lovemaking he'd enjoyed and of future delights yet to come. He returned to the temple that evening, and the next and the next several after that. He enjoyed Celeste's company once more, along with that of Venus and Diana, and the contents of the washstand were no longer a mystery for him. It was like an addiction he couldn't get enough of — until one day when he opened his money pouch to take out the coins required to purchase his entrance ticket.

It felt somewhat light. Nathan counted the golden guineas remaining and swallowed hard. More than half of the funds handed to him by his father to cover his expenses while in Edinburgh were gone — and they had been more than generous. He would not ask for more. He didn't regret the manner in which his coins had been spent. How could he when they had made a man of him? But there would be no more expensive visits to the temple, he decided. On the wall, a framed pen-and-ink sketch of Edinburgh Castle caught his eye. He picked up his hat and gloves and set out to view the castle in person.

Chapter Two

The Kerr coach entered Edinburgh by way of the West Port and Evanna peered out of its window wide-eyed. Beside her, her mama and twin sisters, Marietta and Catriona — a year her junior chattered on. Words like gloomy, big, dirty and smelly were bandied about. Edinburgh might be called 'The Athens of the North', but it couldn't be called over healthy. Evanna ignored them. This was exciting and she intended to enjoy every moment of her time there. Even if, despite her best efforts, it didn't result in a husband. It might be the only chance she got to be part of society, and if she had to return home unwed at least she would have had fun along the way, although she thought she'd best keep that possible conclusion to herself.

When they arrived at Canongate, Evanna could hardly believe her eyes. Apart from being constructed from the same dark grey granite, Acheson House, their rented home for the length of their visit, was as different from Kerr Castle as could be. Tall and narrow at three stories high above ground, the windows of a fourth-floor basement were just visible peeping up from below street level. After the rambling familiarity of Kerr Castle, it was strangely quaint and welcoming.

Beside her, the twins tried to look in all directions at once and talked nineteen to the dozen about what they could see.

"Look, Evanna. That's a man carrying a tray of pies on his head."

"Do you see that beautiful horse?"

"Oh, a park."

"How Robina would love this," Evanna said. The youngest of their siblings, much to her eleven-year-old disgust, had been deemed too young to attend the festivities, so had been left at Kerr Castle in the care of her governess. She had sulked, cried and begged her parents to relent, until Evanna promised her a present if she was good.

It had worked, but Evanna feared Miss McPheat, the governess, was going to have her work cut out.

Papa had undertaken the journey mounted on his favourite stallion, riding alongside the vehicle. Prior to their departure, he had talked enthusiastically about Musselburgh, which Evanna understood to be where the Edinburgh racecourse was located. It sounded as if they would see little of him. Not that it mattered — he was often absent, and she had frequently thought life was more peaceful at those times.

Whether he was resigned to spending his money or not, Evanna had no idea. What she did know was that to her delight she was to be the recipient of several new gowns, and trimmings. Two pairs of silk stockings, the cape and the fringed shawl resided in her trunk along with new petticoats and nightgowns all fashioned by her sisters' clever fingers from the lawns and linens they'd found in Great Grandma's trunk.

"She'd soon be bored," their mama said firmly, speaking about Robina. "And we all know what she is like when she does not have enough to occupy her. She is better off at home."

The words 'where we will not be bothered by her antics' were implied. It was true Robina tended to whine on occasion.

"Now," Mama said as the coach drew to a halt. "Gather up your immediate belongings, girls. The servants will bring your trunks and valises. Tonight will be spent quietly at home, tomorrow we will get our bearings."

Evanna swallowed hard and squashed the excitement rising within her. She would have pinched herself if her mama hadn't been about. Mama was as sharp as a knife about things she called indelicate or unladylike.

Which reminded her of the last ultimatum given to her — the diktat that under no circumstances was she to use her left hand to eat or greet anyone. It was for her reticule and or prayerbook only. As a member of the Kerr clan, who were notoriously caurie-fisted, it was not an easy thing to remember. Recollections of her governess tying her left arm to her waist, and of varied punishments that followed any transgressions, made her shudder, but it was a still an effort not to instinctively use it. Her handwriting was, as one governess put it, akin to a spider dipping its legs in ink then crawling all over the vellum. Very hard to decipher. If no one was around or likely to come across her, Evanna would use her left hand to write fair copy, but always with one eye over her shoulder. To be caught would see her labelled as a freak, an abnormality of nature, which seemed somewhat unfair when the fighting men of the clan were encouraged to use their weapons left handed to maintain an element of surprise over the enemy.

While in Edinburgh though, she'd do her best to be a dutiful daughter. Evanna exited the coach after her mother and sisters and glanced around with interest until sharply spoken to by her parent, to 'come along, do'. She sighed and picked up her skirts to walk up the several steps to the front door, where a very proper major-domo bowed his welcome. She murmured the conventional greetings expected and entered the hall where a middle-aged woman introduced herself as Mrs McHarg, the housekeeper.

The senior servant bobbed a curtsey and spoke deferentially to Lady Kerr, "Your personal rooms are arranged as you requested my lady, and Maisie is waiting to escort your daughters to theirs."

Evanna glanced at the freckle-faced young maid and wondered how her mama had decided how the bedchambers should be allocated. She didn't have long to wonder. Within five minutes, Maisie showed her into what was called the Crimson Room, and "the second-best bedchamber, miss. Your lady mother has the best of course, your father the one decorated as befitting a man."

Evanna wondered what *befitting a man* meant exactly. She chose not to query the statement—that would show her not to be at all up to snuff—and looked around the room. It was a lot smaller than her draughty bedchamber in the castle, which meant it would at least be warm. "This is perfect," she said sincerely. "I will enjoy sleeping here."

Maisie beamed. "There's a withdrawing room next door." She reddened and said in a rush, "with a cludgie in it an all... Just for you an' no sharin', miss." She put her hand over her mouth. "Please dinnae tell Mrs

McHarg I said that. She's always tellin' me nae to be coarse. A… A…commode."

Evanna nodded gravely as she struggled not to grin. "I use cludgie for the facilities as well, Maisie. And, believe me, it's a treat not to have a gardyloo under the bed *and* sharing all the rest with my sisters." She laughed. "And frequently my youngest sister's pet ferret." She never forgot the first time she'd gone to use the chamber pot to discover Hector the ferret fast asleep in it. "He adopted it—unused of course—as his personal sleeping quarters."

Maisie giggled behind her hand. "Ohh, miss, how did you cope?"

"We got another gardyloo and kept it in a cupboard."

* * * *

The thought of Hector and Robina was enough for Evanna to feel somewhat homesick for the familiarity of the castle as she climbed into bed. The feeling only intensified when her bedchamber felt airless and stuffy compared to her draughty sleeping quarters at home. She clambered to her feet once more and set the window ajar. The night air was balmy but still, the slight draught was cooler than the overheated atmosphere inside.

She soon discovered another household close-by must have had the same idea after she settled back down. The tinkling notes of a pianoforte accompanied by the soft hum of voices drifted in and Evanna found the noise soothing. It was a happy sound, she decided. With a gentle buzz of people enjoying themselves, and in a bed softer and more opulent than she was used to, she soon fell asleep.

When she woke in the morning refreshed and ready for her visit to the establishment of Madame Coeur, modiste, she made a mental note to inform her mama of the superiority of the mattress over the one she had at the castle.

Or maybe not, for if her mama decided her own mattress was not so luxurious, Evanna could end up having to swap. She'd keep quiet and enjoy the unaccustomed luxury.

And now she had the added excitement of buying some new gowns.

Evanna discovered from Maisie that Madame Coeur was rumoured to have fled France to avoid the guillotine and come to Edinburgh in memory of the 'Auld Alliance'. A dark-haired petite lady with twinkling eyes which belied her outwardly stern demeanour, she inspected each lady carefully, then nodded. "My lady, your daughters are elegant, but this one" — she touched Evanna on the shoulder — "this one will be the belle of the ball."

Heat rushed into Evanna's cheeks and Madame Coeur beamed. "Ah, perfect, also unaware. How delightful. Now let us begin."

What followed was a flurry of discussions over colours, materials and styles. Consultations over how many of what was considered the minimum number of items to purchase and when they would be ready to be collected. By the time they left, several hours later, Evanna's head was reeling but she was confident that Madame Coeur knew what she was doing. The gown that was to be created for her to wear that evening was, in her mind, the epitome of understated elegance.

She could only hope others would think so as well.

They exited the modiste's establishment and stood for a second on the pavement as Button, the coachman, let down the steps and helped her mama in. Evanna stood back to let her sisters precede her and glanced down the road. How she would love to walk and discover some of the city's fine architecture and parks.

However, it was not to be. She took a step back for one last look at the inspiring outline of the castle and an elegantly dressed young gentleman crossed her eye line. *Perfection personified.*

The prospect of her upcoming evening engagement took on a rosy glow. Perhaps he would be there? She very much hoped so, especially when she twirled in front of her mirror a few hours later dressed in the first-ever formal evening gown she'd ever possessed.

Madam Coeur had worked wonders in short time to create a confection of pale blue satin with tiers of ruffles at its hem that swished delightfully as Evanna swayed. The scooped neckline, lower than would be deemed seemly on a day dress, showed a hint of décolletage which, teamed with the long, silk evening gloves she wore, made her feel rather sophisticated and not a little daring.

Still, Evanna found it hard to appear insouciant when she followed her mama into the Assembly Rooms. Butterflies danced in her stomach and her palms were clammy inside the elegant white gloves. She tried not to appear the country bumpkin and stare around, but it was difficult. She had never expected such grandeur, and she had been told Edinburgh did not reach the height of the magnificence of the ton in London. Surely that could not be true? Nothing could be more stunning than this?

The rooms were ablaze with candles and scented with flowers. The deep red hues of the silk and velvet curtains glittered and shone in the flickering light and the whole vista was one of gaiety and excitement.

Evanna surreptitiously scanned the room and admired the myriad colours and materials of the dresses of the ladies. "How Marietta and Catriona would have enjoyed this, Mama. I wish they were here. It seems cruel not to let them experience the occasion."

"Evening parties are for you alone," her mama replied firmly. "Their time will come once we have you established."

Established. Evanna's heart sank. That sounded… ominous. What if no gentleman liked her demeanour? Or she did not take to them? What then? Would she be the one left at home while the others socialised, or was Papa determined to follow the old adage of eldest first and make the rest wait for their turn? She hoped not. That put the onus on her even more heavily. Failure to make an impression would have repercussions for more than just herself.

However, she had no time to dwell on her fears. A tall, imposing lady approached them and kissed her mama on the cheek.

"My dear Donaldina, how perfect to see you here. I am so glad you were able to attend. And this must be Evanna?"

Donaldina? She'd never heard her mama called that. She knew it was one of her baptismal names, of course, but had thought it was despised and ignored. How interesting to hear it now, and her mama not object. Lady Kerr didn't appear at all fazed though, and returned the salutation with a murmured, "Mhairi, how lovely. Thank you for inviting us."

Evanna knew her etiquette and curtsied dutifully. "Ma'am." What if she was a lady, or more? That would be a very terrible social solecism. It couldn't be helped, though. She had no information to direct her. Her curtsey was, she hoped, the perfect depth and degree of deference to an unknown older female.

"Positively delightful," the woman, Mhairi, said. "I'm not the host per se, just one of the organisers."

"Well, you have done us proud. It is an honour to be invited thus."

"Glad you think so. Better make it worth your while, eh?" Mhairi turned to Evanna. "Now, who should we introduce you to?"

Evanna felt hot then cold. Could she not at least get her bearings first? She had no clue as to what the correct reply should be so answered nervously, "I'm not sure... Who would you suggest?"

Mhairi beamed at her. "Well..."

"I would suggest myself," a new deep voice said before Mhairi could expand on her answer. "My lovely sister here will vouch for me." An older and neatly dressed man with dark hair, greying at the temples kissed their hostess' hand.

"Wilbur," Mhairi spoke with fond exasperation. "I thought you had ridden south, home to Corbridge."

"I did, but business has called me north once more. My arrival yielded the discovery of your having arranged a soiree to which I haven't had an invitation. I presumed I was welcome though, so here I am, and I find you with the most interesting lady in the room."

Mhairi shook her head in mock reproof then looked at Evanna. "My dear Miss Kerr, may I present my brother to your notice? Wilbur Percival-Smyth, who I assumed was over the border. Wilbur, this is Miss Kerr, the daughter of one of my oldest friends."

As any genteel gentleman would do, he bowed to her mama before he turned to Evanna. She curtsied once more and took the chance to take a better look at the man in front of her without appearing bold or forward. He was quite a lot older than she, possibly of more advanced years than either of her parents and his face, although smiling, was unfortunately *not* one to make any young lady's heart beat faster. However, she noticed several other young ladies staring enviously in their direction, so he must be seen as a gentleman of interest. And he had chosen to single her out.

She wasn't sure if that notion was appealing or appalling.

He bowed to her.

Such a lot of bowing and curtseying… It must get very wearing after a while.

"Wilbur Percival-Smyth, entirely at your service," the gentleman informed her. "May I invite you to take a turn around the room with me? All proper and above board, I assure you."

The rather careful enunciation of his words gave tell that the maturity of Mr Percival-Smyth's years *were* considerably more than her own. Evanna glanced at her mama for guidance as to whether his invitation should be accepted or politely turned aside. Lady Kerr smiled encouragingly and nodded her affirmative.

"That is very generous of you, sir, and most acceptable. My daughter will be delighted to join you. Just a short stroll, you understand."

"But of course." He held out his arm. "Miss Kerr?"

"That would be lovely, thank you." She placed her hand properly on his arm and permitted him to steer her across the crowded room, a small thrill dancing down her spine.

She, Evanna Kerr, was with a gentleman who appeared to be most eligible. Oh, she might not be interested in him as a husband, in fact she was sure she wasn't, but it was rather special to be singled out and the envy of others. It was hard to ignore the envious glances thrown her way, and she wouldn't be human not to feel a little smug. After all, it was the first time in her life anything like it had happened, and it might never happen again, so she might as well enjoy it.

They had not taken so many steps when she saw him. The same young man she had noted in the vicinity of the castle while she'd been out shopping that morning. Her heart missed a beat as she noted how perfectly his jacket fitted across his shoulders. Beneath it he wore a green-and-grey-striped waistcoat she found very much to her taste. He paused mid-step and, when their eyes met, he blushed a little, as if he'd seen the admiration in her glance. Then, with apparent disregard for the usual proprieties, he spoke to her without first seeking a formal introduction.

"Ma'am, Miss, I er…um… Na…Nathaniel McColl at your service."

Evanna did not mind his ignoring convention one jot. He was at her service?

Oh, I do hope so.

At her side, her escort bowed but refrained from presenting her by name. "My lord. A pleasure. But you'll excuse us if we don't dally? The supper table beckons."

Lord Whoever nodded his acceptance with a smile, but as they walked away Mr Percival-Smyth was not so complimentary. "The son of a duke in the Assembly Rooms. What on earth is he doing here? I don't understand why he's not in London at this time of the year, but if any young miss in this room thinks to capture him as husband, she'll be sadly mistaken. His father will be looking higher than some provincial nobody for his heir to sire his grandchildren upon."

Evanna felt at a loss as to how to answer Mr Percival-Smyth's dismissive comments on what appeared to her to be a perfectly polite and well-mannered gentleman. Plus, his opinion of the young ladies in the room, of whom she was one, she found equally unpalatable. She had detected no untoward condescension from the son of a duke to the high rank of his station but wished she'd paid a little more attention to his name rather than his waistcoat, so ventured to enquire in what she hoped was in an insouciant manner. "I do not know many people in Edinburgh as yet. I haven't to date come across Lord ah…did he say, Mc something?"

Mr Percival-Smyth patted her hand. "Very sensible of you not to fawn over him, nor honour him with undue attention he has done nothing to earn bar the fact of his being born noble. He is Lord McColl or, to give him his full title, Viscount Nathanial McColl, son and heir of the Duke of Glenard. Come to visit his godfather, Sir Douglas Wallace, I've been given to understand."

Chapter Three

Nathan stood, transfixed, as he stammered his name to the stunningly pretty brunette in front of him and fought not to blurt out instead what was uppermost in his mind.

Why are you with that dry old stick?

Alain had pointed the man out to him when they'd entered the Assembly Rooms earlier in the evening. A canny merchant who'd turned his business into a small empire. As rich as Croesus, Percival-Smyth was an alderman of the up-and-coming town of Corbridge who had the reputation of having a finger in every pie, including several particularly tasty ones in the Scottish capital.

Damn it!

Worse, Nathan had thought his time in the temple of love had given him a certain ease when in the company of a beautiful woman—but not this one it seemed. She had literally taken his breath away, and he cursed himself for blushing and stuttering like a plebeian fool. How gauche she must think him. He thought perhaps there had been a glimmer of interest in her eyes, but had he imagined it?

Nathan set his mind to finding out, but his attempts to do so met with little success. The Assembly Rooms were beautifully appointed but stuffily overpopulated with more persons than was comfortable—a situation that did not improve when the first cotillion was called. The centre of the floor emptied for the dancers to take their places, leaving those promenading around its outer edges in even closer proximity.

He caught the occasional glimpse of the lady of his dreams during the evening, but, despite his best efforts, he failed to reach her—and it was not solely due to the overcrowding, but rather that his way toward her was barred by one determined mama after another begging to present him with their daughter's name. Good manners dictated he accept the introduction to each blushing young lady before excusing himself with smiling good grace, until he was sure he could feel dagger-like stares on his back whenever he turned away, for he had asked none of them to dance.

Eventually he managed to make his way to Alain's side and found his friend looking thoroughly fed up. "I've literally been bumped from pillar to post in this melee. I'm guessing the full moon has encouraged more guests to turn out than is usual. The supper table should still be laid up at home. Shall we take our leave?"

Nothing loath to depart, Nathan nodded. Several other persons seemed to have had the same idea, and as he and Alain walked towards the door, he was thrilled to see the prize he had been seeking all evening. Close enough to catch her eye, he made her a small bow of acknowledgement. The brilliant smile she returned to him was delightful, as was the impish dimple that appeared beside her mouth. Her companion spoke.

"Evanna, kindly stop grinning like a Cheshire cat. It is most unseemly. Now, do come along. You have an arrangement to take the air with your sisters in the park come the morning if the weather remains fine."

The dimple deepened at the scolding. Nathan's own smile widened to match the animal named then the dark-haired beauty straightened her face and complied to the instruction given. "Yes, Mama."

Evanna...

Nathan rolled her name around on his tongue as he watched the two ladies depart. An engagement to attend the cock pit the following morning suddenly lost its appeal.

The park. Yes. That's the thing.

Alain's interested gaze also followed the two ladies as they left the room. "Beautiful girl. Who are they?"

His question surprised Nathan. "You don't know them?"

Alain shook his head. "No. Not a clue. They must be new to town. M'father will know if any visitors worthy of note have recently arrived in the city, though."

* * * *

Alain's assumption proved correct as, when they were seated at the table with a large slice of game pie apiece in front of them an hour later, Alain gave a brief description and posed the question.

Sir Douglas contemplated the matter while he chewed and answered after he swallowed. "Could be Lord and Lady Kerr. They've recently arrived in the city with a bevy of daughters. All exceptionally pretty girls, apparently. They've rented a place on Cannongate for a couple of months. Acheson House."

Nathan nearly choked on his mouthful of pie. *Acheson House? The residence next door to the temple of love?*

He side-eyed Alain, who grinned but refrained from comment. However, there must have been something perhaps a little too eager in Nathan's expression when the Kerr name had been mentioned, for his godfather looked directly at him and continued, "Your father entrusted you to my care, so in his absence it behoves me to offer any necessary paternal advice. A beautiful girl will always command attention, but you need to beware of raising false expectations. Be polite, be charming, discover which compliments appeal to a young lady and which do not, but coolly, at a distance. By all means, take the opportunity to garner a little of the social ease you will require when you come of age next year and visit London for the Season, but daughters of the minor nobility are not for the likes of you. Sons of dukes owe it to their family lineage to marry higher in the order than a mere miss. The daughter of an earl should be your minimum requirement but given your future title a princess from a minor European principality is not beyond your reach."

Nathan squirmed, uncomfortable at this pronouncement. Knowing what he did now from his time in the temple he didn't much fancy performing the physical act of love with a bride rejected by suitors of royal blood, probably for being squint-eyed or some such thing. Like Alain, he refrained from making any reply that might cause the temple to be brought into the discussion, and his discomfort increased when next Sir Douglas turned his attention to his son.

"For you, though, the eldest daughter of Lord and Lady Kerr would be a most suitable match. You are both of equable station, young, and in good health. That she is beautiful should make the prospect highly palatable…" Sir Douglas pushed his chair away from the table and stood. "And on that note, I'll leave you gentlemen to chew over my advice. Think carefully and choose wisely. Good night."

The door closed behind Sir Douglas' retreating figure. Alain wrinkled his nose and spoke airily to the back of it. "The trouble is, I'm rather enjoying my bachelorhood and have no intention of exchanging it for the married state any time soon, be it with the lovely Miss Kerr or anyone else."

Relief flooded Nathan's frame. "You haven't?"

Alain poured each of them another glass of wine. "No. I rather have a fancy to accompany you to London next year. If you'll have me?"

The thought of having a firm friend at his side when tackling the intricacies of the *haut ton* was reassuringly welcome, and Nathan raised his glass in a toast to his friend. "I'd be nothing but delighted."

The matter agreed upon, they finished their wine and parted ways outside their respective bedroom doors. Nathan instructed his valet to wake him in good time for his outing to the park then spent a dream-filled night kissing a pair of lips that had a certain dimple by their side.

* * * *

Evanna opened the window before she climbed into bed and found their near neighbours must be more hospitable than most when she heard the same combination of music and conversation as she had the previous night. She blew out the candle and cast her mind over everything that had occurred during the evening while relaxing to the sound.

She had achieved some small success, she thought. Her dance card had soon been filled, and her partners had proved flatteringly attentive. Then there was Lord Nathaniel McColl. She conjured up his handsome face and smiled. She'd hoped he would ask her to dance and had been disappointed when he hadn't — until the end of the evening, when he'd looked directly into her eyes and bowed. So charming and more meaningful than mere polite gesture, surely? Especially when added to the broad smiles they'd exchanged at Mama scolding her.

Perhaps she would encounter him in the park in the morning. The thought was enough for her body to tingle. Would he bow, or maybe even take her hand and kiss it? How would she respond?

Properly of course, but if she could, she would find a way to show *him* how interested she was in return. And that brought another not-so-welcome interested party to mind.

Percival-Smyth. She frowned. Mama had been nothing but delighted at his overtures, but there was something about the man Evanna found rather off-putting.

His age? That certainly was not a factor in his favour. Then there was a certain unsavoury expression she'd glimpsed out of the corner of her eye when he'd thought she wasn't looking. She could only liken it to the time she'd witnessed the barn cat at home stalk a mouse and trap it in a corner where its final fate was largely inevitable. Faintly triumphant but also a little greedy as it prepared to enjoy its snack.

I feel like the mouse.

That thought was *definitely* not appealing, and neither were the disparaging words he uttered with regards to the ladies in the room *and* Nathaniel.

That was perhaps the biggest black mark against him.

It was a pity her mama was so enamoured with him, and his interest in her eldest daughter. She had crowed about it until Evanna was nigh on ready to scream.

"Your father will be so pleased. Fancy, Evanna, a man like him, so personable, taking an interest in you."

"He was being polite, Mama, after his sister introduced us. No more. I am much too young for the likes of him."

"Rubbish. An older man is so much more… accommodating and knows how to go on." Her mother had waggled her finger. *"No need to be coy, my love. He could not take his eyes off you. So many young ladies trying to attract his attention and he was having nothing of it. Perhaps he is even now preparing to speak to your papa."*

"I hope not," Evanna had said without thinking. *"I'm sorry, Mama, but he is too mature in years and, I think, rather too sure of himself."* She had winced at the astonished – and annoyed – expression on her mama's face.

"What?" Her mama had nigh on screeched the word. *"Don't be silly and waste this opportunity. Mr Percival-Smyth is a warm man who gave you every attention. Do you not realise what a catch he is? You didn't even have to try to attach him. I'm sure he will intend to court you properly, but oh my…"*

What a revolting expression. Catch him indeed.

"I have no intention of trying to catch anyone, Mama."

Especially him.

"I don't want to be seen as fast or flighty for setting my cap at a man in such an obvious manner…" She had

paused. *"So it might be best if I'm not seen with Mr Percival-Smyth too often."*

"Pshaw. Do not be missish. You must encourage him discreetly. Show you are interested without being forward."

"But I'm not interested," Evanna had said with quiet dignity. Really, her mama was impossible in this mood.

"Balderdash," her mother had replied as she'd waggled her finger, admonishing Evanna. *"You should be, my girl. If you let a prospect like him slip through your fingers your father will not be best pleased. We're not made of money, and this is your chance."*

A chance she'd prefer not to have, Evanna decided, as she remembered how her mama had stalked out and banged the door behind her. She sighed. Perhaps it would have been better if she'd stayed at Kerr Castle.

But then I wouldn't have met Lord McColl.

Evanna tweaked the coverlet up over her shoulder and closed her eyes. Her first social outing in Edinburgh had given her much food for thought — but it had only been the first. She was here for several weeks. There was no need for her to express a preference for one particular man over another with such haste, surely? She recalled Lord McColl's face to mind and drifted off to sleep…

* * * *

Only to be woken by an excited Maisie, who shook her gently and told her a gentleman had called.

"Eh?" Only half-awake, Evanna took several seconds to absorb the information. "A gentleman? Who?" Her heart missed a beat. Could it have been *him*?

Maisie soon put paid to that idea.

"Not so much a gentleman," Maisie said cheerily as she handed Evanna a mug of chocolate. "More like a gentleman's gentleman. That Mr Percival-Smyth's man. He's brought an invitation from his master. Oh, miss, isn't it exciting?"

Exciting? Evanna thought the exact opposite but didn't voice it. "I'm due to walk in the gardens with my sisters before lunch," she said. "Have any packages arrived for me from Madame Coeur?"

If Maisie thought it strange her mistress didn't comment on the missive from Mr Percival-Smyth she was wise enough not to say so. "Yes, miss. I was going to bring them up directly."

A thought lingered.

Viscount McColl might be at the park. I must look at my best.

Evanna smiled. "There should be a lemon floral day gown. The one with daisies embroidered around the hem and sleeves. Lay it out for me, if you will?"

Maisie bobbed a curtsey in acknowledgement of the request then left the room. Evanna sipped her chocolate when the door closed behind her maid and considered her options. Mr Percival-Smyth was obviously an important personage it would not be wise to offend. Should she meet him in the park her demeanour would be polite but distant, but should she encounter Lord McColl, the warmth of her smile would hopefully alert him to the fact that his company was more than welcome.

Maisie returned, and, once dressed, Evanna descended the stairs to find the twins waiting for her, both looking as pleased as punch in their newly refurbished bonnets.

"See, Evanna, aren't they pretty?"

"No one will have bonnets as beautiful as ours."

Evanna smiled. One of Great Grandma's more ornate evening gowns had yielded a quantity of finely worked pink silk roses. Mama had gifted them to Marietta and Catriona, who had used them to adorn their hats. "You both look lovely."

Lady Kerr appeared from the direction of the dining room with Maisie in tow and issued her final instructions. "Now remember, you girls walk together with Maisie following behind…" She fixed Evanna with a pointed look. "But should a certain *gentleman of quality* wish to converse with Evanna, you younger girls will drop back and walk with Maisie while keeping Evanna and her beau in sight. Luncheon is at one. Be home before it. Mr Percival-Smyth has kindly sent round tickets for us to attend a musicale performance at Lady Escot's later this afternoon. Very exclusive. Signora LaTesca is to entertain us with a selection of Mozart's finest arias."

Oh, tarnation! Not him again. Is the wretched man to dog my footsteps every single day?

* * * *

Nathaniel completed a second circuit of the park then glanced at his fob watch only to find not twenty minutes had passed since he'd last done so. He continued to stroll, taking care to nod gracefully at any acquaintance he recognised without catching their eye, thereby negating the obligation to pause for a minute or two of polite conversation. By this method, he hoped, when Evanna entered the park, he would be unburdened by other company and free to approach her.

He walked on, glancing left and right before assaying a rueful smile — if he hadn't been so anxious not to miss Evanna, he would have been amused at his antics. Not even Celeste and his sexual education had tied him in knots like the thought of seeing Evanna had. A few more paces and his efforts were finally rewarded. The sight he had been waiting for came into view. Three young ladies passed through the park gates accompanied by a maid walking several proper paces behind them. His heart missed a beat. A vision in a yellow day dress dotted with flowers grew steadily clearer. Evanna and her sisters were walking sedately towards him.

How should he act?

For goodness' sake, man. Be yourself.

Evanna glanced towards him so he smiled and was delighted to see her dimple appear as she dropped a curtsey and held out her hand as she straightened. "Lord McColl. Well met."

Without thinking, he took her hand and brushed his lips over the back of it to an audible intake of breath from the other two young ladies accompanying her. Her dimple deepened, and he hastily smothered a reciprocal grin to utter an appropriate greeting. "Miss Kerr, how lovely to see you and your charming companions."

She retrieved her hand from his and introduced them. "My younger sisters, Marietta and Catriona."

As alike as two peas in a pod, there was no clue as to which was which, so Nathan bowed to each of them in turn. "Enchanted." Then asked Evanna, "May I be so bold as to stroll and enjoy the air with you for a while?"

"That, my lord," she replied with a twinkle in her eyes that delighted him, "would be both an honour and a privilege."

"I assure you, Miss Kerr," he said in a voice that even though he fought to disguise it held a hint of elation, "the honour and privilege is mine."

They walked side by side and Nathan found the conversation flowed easily. They both admired the cultivated neatness of the park's floral beds. In full bloom, roses and marigolds were set into ornate patterns unobtainable in the windswept heather-strewn wilderness of the Scottish countryside. This, in turn, led to their talking of their childhood homes. Kerr Castle located in the Cheviot Hills near the border between Scotland and England, and his own sprawling ducal pile farther north near Loch Lomond in the Trossachs.

Several aspects of their childhoods proved similar — freezing draughts that were impossible to escape in a castle during winter, roaring fires and waking to the water in the ewer having turned to ice in the morning — all offset by spectacular scenery and the glorious blanket of purple of Scotland's national plant when the air finally warmed in mid-to-late summer. So comfortable did he feel that he plucked up the courage to steer their exchange down a slightly more personal path.

"Having no siblings, I always wondered what it would be like to do so. Was your sisters' companionship as beneficial as my imagination would have me believe?"

Evanna took a quick glance over her shoulder at the girls walking behind them. "For the most part, yes. We love each other dearly, but the twins are not just identical in looks, they also think alike and often have no need of company bar their own. Robina is still only eleven, then there was my unfortunate — " A discreet cough sounded behind them and Evanna paused mid-sentence. "I fear we best be getting back. We are due to attend Lady Escot's musicale later today. Will you be there? Signora LaTesca is to sing."

Nathaniel had been sent a ticket, of course. It was on his mantel with a myriad of others—the son of a duke was to be invited to every event taking place in town whether he had a passing acquaintance with the hosts or not, it appeared. Up until that moment he'd had no intention of accepting it but now…

"Of course," he said promptly. "I will hope to see you there." He bowed, took his leave of all three ladies and with a jaunty swing of his cane headed to his godfather's house. He needed to change into the proper attire required to attend a musicale and possibly find something to put in his ears—discreetly, of course—for when Signora LaTesca sang. For he was no aficionado of opera.

* * * *

Evanna stood on tiptoes and glanced around the room, only half paying attention to Mr Percival-Smyth, who had approached her and Mama as soon as they had entered the long, brightly lit room where the musicale was to be performed.

"My dear Miss Kerr. Well met. May I invite you to take a glass of ratafia with me when the interval is called?"

She answered quickly to circumvent the possibility of Mama stepping in and accepting on her behalf. "How kind, but I am afraid you are too late."

Her mother's lips thinned, and Evanna guessed she was in for a telling off later, unless…

Find an alternative. One that won't leave me alone with him.

"However, perhaps you will be at the museum on Thursday? They are holding an open afternoon."

Lady Kerr's expression relaxed somewhat, although Mr Percival-Smyth looked faintly appalled. "Well, ah…"

"The event is perhaps not to your taste?" she asked, trying to keep the hope from her voice.

His reply dashed that aspiration instantly. "For you, my dear, I will go against my inclinations. I would be delighted to escort you."

Tarnation! However, it appears it is the lesser of two evils.

"Then, may I introduce you to my sisters, Marietta and Catriona? We are all to attend. They are so looking forward to it."

His smile dimmed when Evanna imparted that particular piece of information, and somewhat stiffly, he bowed in their direction. "It will be an honour to escort both you and your sisters. Shall we say Thursday at two?" The small orchestra began to tune their instruments, giving her no need to reply, so she curtsied her acceptance and took her seat.

The twins, as ever bolstered by each other's company, exhibited no sign of the nerves that had assailed Evanna on her first public outing to the Assembly Rooms the previous evening. Less than a minute after they took their seats, they began to whisper and giggle behind their hands.

"Oh, do look at the lady in blue."

"Those ribbons are rather overdone for an afternoon gown, don't you think?"

"There's Evanna's beau from the park yesterday."

Evanna felt a nudge in her ribs.

"Why is everyone staring at him?"

Summoning the decorum that wouldn't be expected from two young girls not yet *out*, she resisted the urge to swivel in her chair, although it didn't stop her heart beating faster. "I have no idea and it would be unseemly for me to turn and look."

Catriona wrinkled her nose. "Why? How else will you find out?"

"I won't. Now hush, the pair of you, it is rude to stare and comment so obviously while awaiting the performance. Be careful or Mama may deem you too young to attend anything else." She ignored the two gasps of horror and settled deep into her chair. Mama had left the seat between them empty and was busy chatting to one of her cronies. Evanna crossed her fingers and hoped Mr Percival-Smyth, talking to his sister on the far side of the room, wouldn't notice the vacant seat then to her relief, he took a chair several rows in front of her.

Which made it all the better, when with a hurried "excuse me, is this seat taken or may I occupy it?", Lord Nathan McColl sat down and smiled. "Oh, Miss Kerr, I didn't realise it was you," he said in such a pseudo-sincere voice she bit her lip so as not to grin. "And your sisters are with you too, I see."

"Indeed, they are, my lord." *Please invite me to spend the interval in your company.*

"May I escort you to the refreshments?"

Praise be! "I would be delighted."

"Excellent." The orchestra rose to their feet and bowed as a statuesque brunette swept into the room. With the ghost of a mischievous wink, Lord McColl twitched two small pieces of linen from his pocket, rolled them into small balls and popped one in each ear. "This is our prima donna, I believe. So, until then…"

It was all Evanna could do to restrain the giggles that threatened to burst forth at the look of resigned horror that passed over his face as the notes of the opening overture sounded.

Chapter Four

Nathan couldn't believe his luck. Not only an empty seat next to Miss Kerr, but she wasn't engaged for the interval. He crossed one leg over the other in what he hoped was an elegant pose and positioned his body a little sideways on his seat so the beautiful profile of the lady beside him filled his eyeline rather than the staged scene to the front of him.

La Tosca opened her mouth and her glass-shattering soprano, delightfully muffled to him, filled the room. Miss Kerr's eyebrows shot up as her ears were assaulted and Nathan nearly chuckled. Their appreciation of the opera was the same, it seemed. He should have brought two additional pieces of linen with him.

The interval was called sixty wearying minutes later, and Miss Kerr's delightful dimple appeared when he twitched the material from his ears. He stood and smiled at her. "Shall we?"

Lady Kerr sat straighter, and her gaze darted around the room. "Evanna... I believe you are engaged for the next few minutes..."

Miss Kerr jumped to her feet. "I am, Mama. Lord McColl has kindly invited me to take a turn round the room with him."

"But, but...Mr Percival..."

"Will not be short of other company, I'm sure."

Lady Kerr looked none too pleased, and he wondered why, when every other mama in the room seemed determined to catch his eye.

* * * *

This viewpoint was only reinforced when two days later his godfather introduced him to Lord Kerr at the gentleman's New Club that gathered at Bayle's Tavern on Princes Street.

Lord Kerr bowed. "You're newly arrived in town, my lord?"

Nathan nodded his assent and Lord Kerr looked him up and down in a manner Nathan found bordering on rude. "Got the young ladies hanging on your every word, I daresay. If you'll take the advice of one more wise to the world, take care how much attention you pay 'em..." The man's stare became more pointed. "Don't give 'em false expectations."

The man's presumption left Nathan momentarily speechless, and more so an hour later when he overheard a conversation about him that was very obviously not meant for his ears.

"Over-young. A couple more years or three will be needed for him to be up to snuff as husband material, and in the meantime, I don't want him dangling after my daughter. She's here for marriage, not casual dalliance." Lord Kerr nudged his companion and gave him a sly wink. "Now, Mr Percival-Smyth is a different matter altogether. Mature, established, well setup..."

"Percival-Smyth's courting your daughter?"

Lord Kerr puffed out his chest. "Smitten, my wife informs me. Evanna is nigh on spoken for..."

Nathan bowed and turned away.

Insufferable prig! Poor Evanna. Does she know that?

He removed himself from the man's orbit and pondered what to do next. He definitely had feelings for Miss Kerr, and she also appeared to have a tendre for him. He longed to spend more time in her company, and if their feelings deepened, he would prove to her parents he was no flibbertigibbet without serious intentions. His decision made, momentary doubt assailed him. Could she really be interested in a man such as Percival-Smyth, in preference to himself? He would not believe it until he heard it from her own lips.

* * * *

A saunter around the park the following morning gave him hope that an opportunity to do so would be with him that night. Her sisters had paused to admire the scented blooms on a particularly pretty rose bush while Evanna looked on from the path a few yards away. He made his bow, and his heart sang at the sparkle that lit her eyes when she looked directly at him, then offered him her gloved hand.

"Good morning, my Lord."

Oh, that voice, like a nightingale. He brushed his lips over the back of her hand and ventured a small joke.

"Your ears have recovered from the assault they suffered at the soiree yesterday, I hope."

His happiness increased when she took up the gauntlet and answered in kind.

"Thankfully they have, my lord." She laughed, a tinkling happy sound that made him want to capture it and listen to it forever.

How fanciful. Not at all like him. It appeared both his heart *and* mind were affected by her.

"Although, like you," she continued, "I will not attend such an event in future without the boon of two small squares of linen cut from my handkerchief being concealed about my person."

The smile she gave him emboldened him to ask, "Ah... I don't suppose you would care to call me Nathan?"

How forward, but a faint heart never won a lady, or so they say.

Her dimple appeared as she accepted his tentative invitation to deepen their acquaintance. "Between ourselves, I would be happy to. If you would reciprocate by using my given name?"

"Nathan and Evanna it is then," he announced with a touch of theatrical aplomb.

She glanced towards her sisters and giggled. "Nathan! They will hear you." She stuck her nose in the air. "And I'm supposed to be a model of perfect propriety for them. We may be rebuked if it's noticed how free we are with each other."

Her tone was encouragingly light-hearted enough to tell him her words contained no real of censure, so he pushed his luck a touch further. "So, my dear Evanna. Are you attending any soirees today?"

Her eyes sparkled. "We are bound for Lady Macreston's dance this evening. At Leith. Mama says the journey is tedious, but I don't care. We live very quietly at home, and these are the first *real* parties I've been invited to. Will you be there?"

Lady Macreston was one of his late mother's more irritating cronies with a tendency to meddle, and even with her son Cameron being a good friend of his, Nathan had hesitated to accept her invitation—but if Evanna was to attend…?

"I certainly will," he vowed. He hesitated for a second.

Be bold if you do not ask you will not kmow.

Nathan cleared his throat and asked hopefully, "Perhaps there will be an opportunity for us to converse a little more?"

Evanna blushed. "I would like that."

His thoughts whirled—a handy spot where a couple could conduct a little private conversation was not something he'd ever had reason to consider before. "Um… Perhaps if you mark my name on your dance card for the one the before supper we could stroll on the terrace after it?"

Her smile faltered. "Mama has already reserved that particular dance for Mr Percival-Smyth."

His hopes dashed, Nathan could find nothing to say other than a totally inadequate, "Oh…"

She lifted her chin, a determined gleam in her eye. "Mama may push his company on me all she likes, but that does not mean I have to spend every minute of the interval with him. I shall find some reason or other to excuse myself and take a stroll in your company before the music resumes."

Nathan tried to keep the hopeful quaver from his voice. "You do not favour him then?"

She shrugged. "I can claim no more than a passing acquaintance with the man, and from our brief conversations so far, no inclination to know Mr Percival-Smyth any better that I do now. It may be because he's so much older than me, but I have discovered nothing we share in common. Except we are both in Edinburgh at this moment. He may have my mama in his thrall, but she is not me."

Nathan's heart leapt, but as he opened his mouth to urge her to expand on the subject, she took a sudden step backward. A glance sideways explained it. Lady Kerr was bustling down the path in their direction. She acknowledged Nathan's presence with the briefest of nods, then turned a dismissive shoulder to him without so much as even uttering a polite good morning. "Evanna, why are you dallying here? Where are you sisters?"

Evanna blushed, then reminded her parent of her manners with a politeness her mother had failed to display. "Over yonder, looking at the roses, Mama. Viscount McColl happened to stroll by while they did and kindly stopped to enquire whether we were attending Lady Macreston's entertainment this evening."

Presented with his name and title, Lady Kerr could ignore him no longer, although her lips thinned as she was obliged to turn towards him and speak. "I wish you a good day, my lord. We are certainly bound to Lady Macreston's evening entertainment. Isn't everyone? It will be *such* a crush. I'm *sure* Evanna's dance card is already full...but still..."

She gave Nathan a hard stare. "Don't let us keep you." She called her other daughters to order. "Catriona. Marietta. Come attend your sister."

Nathan's cheeks heated at the abruptness of Lady Kerr's manners, but aware of the age difference between himself and the older lady, he was too much of a gentleman to return to her the snub she so richly deserved. Instead, he made the briefest of bows in her direction, turned on his heel and walked away. Lady Kerr's voice followed him on the air.

"I think your dark green gown with the paler green trim would suit this evening's entertainment to perfection, Evanna. I can't wait for a certain *someone* to see you in it. It may be enough for him to show his hand."

"Mama, I'm not sure the gentleman I believe you're referring to and I have anything in common." Evanna's voice held more than a hint of protest. "I don't understand why you and Papa seem determined to foist Mr Percival-Smyth upon me."

A nearby bush offered Nathan the chance to linger unseen and hear more of this exchange. He stepped behind it.

"Things in common? Pish! Kindly stop talking such rubbish, Evanna. You should count yourself lucky I care for you enough to have persuaded Papa to undertake the expense of this visit to the capital so you may meet a gentleman of suitable quality. A man of maturity in possession of the means to be able to provide for a wife is not to be sniffed at."

"But shouldn't there also be shared interests that lead to love?" Evanna said with a quiet dignity Nathan silently applauded.

"Romantic nonsense. Love will avail you nothing. A well-respected man who can afford the expense of the children you will bear him is a superior match to any title, no matter how grand, if the funds are not there."

What a horrible statement.

"Has marriage to Papa made you so cynical, Mama?" Evanna queried. "I never thought of you so."

"What you call cynical, I call practical." Lady Kerr's voice took on a bitter edge. "And while we're conversing frankly on this subject let me add, marriage to a lord comes with certain expectations, and that includes being able to produce an heir to the title. If, like myself, you can only bear girls, then romance, love or whatever you'd like to call it, vanishes in a puff of insubstantial smoke. You have to fight for every penny it takes to raise them. I would not wish it for you."

So that's the lie of the land, is it?

Nathan walked on feeling somewhat reassured. Lady Kerr was entirely correct in her summation of his current financial position. The funds were definitely not in tune, but his father was a generous man, and he was reasonably confident that should he wish to marry a suitable allowance would be forthcoming. And on the subject of any future child of his, she had definitely mistaken her man. He would never shun his wife in such a manner. A daughter between himself and the woman he loved would be adored, and although his father's title would pass to his cousin, there was plenty of unentailed wealth to ensure any child he fathered would be well provided for. Should matters between himself and Evanna come to fruition, all that remained would be to convince his prospective parents-in-law of that.

* * * *

Evanna's spirits dropped as she listened to the cynicism pouring out of her mama's mouth. The hard-nosed views she heard on what constituted a suitable attribute for wedded bliss only strengthened her own stance — a bleak union, such as her parents shared, was not for her. Mutual love and respect in marriage should not be so easily dismissed as unobtainable — they were, as they ever had been, her aim. She was truly sorry her mother had experienced such disappointment in the wedded state, but in Evanna's mind, that was no good reason for the first eligible bachelor that hove into view to be the only and final choice.

Blow Mr Percival-Smyth! What's the rush? We've only been in town for a few days after all.

Such a rebellious outlook would not be looked upon kindly though, so she would keep her own counsel and go her own way regardless without causing a fuss.

Catriona and Marietta finally obeyed their mother's instructions to come hither, and they all walked home together to partake of nuncheon, after which the twins were dispatched to occupy themselves in their room. Mama was officially *at home* for the rest of the afternoon. Evanna assumed the pose of a young lady as social protocol dictated — sitting ramrod straight on the edge of her seat while Mama entertained her visitors in the drawing room.

Half an hour later, she was envying her sisters' escape. Lazing on her bed with a good book would be preferable to the stiffness she was experiencing from maintaining such an unnatural posture. Still, she mustn't complain. Nothing as fine as a formal 'at home' ever took place at Kerr Castle. Visitors generally just called at any old time and took potluck.

The first guest was shown in just as she was contemplating stretching her legs by taking a turn around the room in the hope of glancing out of the window to view whether any activity could be seen on the street.

"Mrs Ponsbury, my lady," their major-domo announced with a flourish.

The friend her mother had named as Mhairi at the Assembly Rooms removed her gloves and looked around her with interest as she sat down. "I've always wondered what the interior of Acheson House was like. Nobody seems to stay very long. I don't why. It seems very comfortable."

"It is," Lady Kerr assured her. "The fixtures and fittings are first rate, and I've found the staff nothing but efficient and willing."

"Something of a mystery then," Mhairi mused. "Your neighbours are people of suitable breeding, I presume?"

"Very respectable so far as I've seen. The carriages that pass up and down the street are of good quality, and the persons I've seen pass by our window have exhibited no aberration of behaviour or manners, although none have yet left their card. I asked our major-domo whether there were any others of title residing nearby and he replied in the negative, so…"

"You cannot call and leave your card with them until they do so here." Mhairi finished for her.

"Exactly. It simply would not *do*." Lady Kerr huffed. "A petty-fogging restriction of rank when I am as curious as the next person as to who my near neighbours could be."

"Irksome, indeed. A title alone is no guarantee of good character. Take my brother for instance…"

"A fine gentleman of the most superior quality, title or no."

Both ladies gazed at her speculatively, and Evanna hurried to divert the conversation away from her least favourite subject. "There must be a hostess of amiable qualities in the house next to this one. I hear her evening parties taking place when I retire to bed each night. Nothing raucous. Just the tinkle of a pianoforte and snatches of soft conversation. All very elegant and genteel."

Mhairi smiled. "Then maybe she will notice the carriages pulling up and realise you're at home today. You should have plenty of visitors calling in to take tea. I put the word around as I promised your dearest mother I would."

A small flush of pleasure stained Lady Kerr's cheeks, and it soon became apparent Mhairi had done an excellent job. Lady Merrythorpe was next to be announced, then a Mrs Murray, followed by pair of middle-aged spinsters, Miss Boothroyd and Miss Lloyd, another young matron, Mrs McVeigh and finally Lady Wallace. The tea tray was rung for, and the talk turned to the entertainment on offer at Lady Macreston's that evening.

Lady Wallace smiled. "I wondered, with the journey to Leith being somewhat tedious, whether the young men of our household would cry off, but they have not. Both our son, Alain, and our houseguest will accompany myself and Sir Douglas to the party. If I may recommend Alain as an accomplish dancer…"

Mrs Murray leant forward to set her teacup down on the table, a speculative gleam in her eye as she cut across Lady Wallace and asked, "Viscount McColl?"

Lady Merrythorpe entered the fray. "A handsome prospect, but not, may I suggest, for a young lady seeking marriage. I take it your daughter Harriet is attending the dance?"

Evanna's mother jumped in and added her two-penny-worth. "A very personable man, but having not yet attained his majority, no young lady should be foolish enough to think he's on the marriage mart." She nodded approvingly at Lady Merrythorpe. "You will take him in hand, my dear?"

Lady Merrythorpe smiled smugly. "At the first opportunity."

Evanna's heart sank to her boots. Having never seen Harriet, she had no idea whether she was a possible rival, but Lady Merrythorpe was exceedingly pretty. It seemed as if every female in the town was queuing up to steal Nathan's attention away from herself. The afternoon lost a little of its shine, and she was nothing but glad when the ladies departed so she could run upstairs to prepare for her evening jaunt.

Her spirits recovered while she relaxed in the luxury of a hot bath—so much easier to arrange in this house than in a castle of spiralling stone stairs where the water was at best tepid by the time it arrived. So far Nathan had showed a distinct preference for her company above that of any other. It was up to her ensure it stayed that way.

Her evening gown, the second of three Mama had commissioned, was to be given its first airing, and Evanna was in awe of the modiste's skill once Maisie fastened it at her back. Madame Coeur had created an exquisite wonder of unstiffened Mulberry silk. Leaf green in colour, the scooped neckline was daringly dipped and the supple fabric, without clinging to her body in an indecent manner that might invite censure, shimmered and swayed with her when she moved. Nature had endowed her with large, firm breasts by the age of fourteen, which had mortified her at the time, but now the full moons peeping out of her bodice made her feel womanly, ready for love. Evanna hoped Nathan would think so too.

A surprise awaited her when she tripped down the stairs at the appointed time. Papa, clothed in his evening apparel, was standing at the foot of them, and for once his scowl was not present. He looked almost benign as he nodded approvingly in her direction.

"You'll do, and I warrant someone else will agree. Mind, no missish airs when Mr Percival-Smyth approaches you. He won't thank you for 'em, nor will I. Cultivate him."

That explained why her father was attending an entertainment he would usually avoid for being akin to spending the evening with toothache. Evanna sighed but held her peace. Mama joined them, and she followed her parents from the house for their journey to Leith on the shores of the River Forth. Several other carriages were heading in the same direction and more than one sporting equipage overtook their transport.

"Young whippersnappers," her father snarled as one such outfit cut in tight in front of them and their coach slowed abruptly. "Need a good talking to."

Evanna smiled into the shadows. Papa's newfound bonhomie at attending a party had proved short-lived. He was back to his normal irascible self.

As she'd suspected, the minute she entered the ballroom Mr Percival-Smyth was at her side, and with both her mother and father encouraging him to do so, there he stayed. Thankfully, he didn't completely overstep the mark by asking her to dance more than twice, but nevertheless, as each new partner escorted her back to her parents, he was standing with them, and his condescending attitude riled her. Could he really think she would take his remarks as a compliment when they contained phrases such as, 'there's a good girl' and 'aren't we looking pretty today'? At one point she would not have held herself completely surprised if he'd patted the top of her head, for all the world as if she were a puppy in training.

Discretion being the better part of valour, Evanna kept her gaze lowered rather than issue the very unladylike retort hovering on the tip of her tongue — until Mr Percival-Smyth excelled himself during supper when he actually presumed to pat her hand without her having given him the least sign of encouragement to do so.

"Your modest manners are to be admired, my dear. They are what I like to see in a woman. The subtle quietness and decorum of your replies tells me you understand men are the superior breed to be deferred to, which suits me perfectly." He paused and gave her a small wink, which did nothing but turn her stomach. "I will say no more here, but soon…"

Evanna looked around, but no help was at hand. Mama had nodded her approval and allowed Mr Percival-Smyth to lead her into supper unchaperoned. Papa, she suspected, had taken his chance to lope off to the card room. She could bear Mr Percival-Smyth's company no longer, so stood. "I thank you for your kindness, sir. However, it will soon be time for the next part of the entertainment, and before it resumes, I'm afraid I must beg your pardon. Please excuse me." She dipped him a small curtsey and headed towards the withdrawing room, ignoring his harumph of displeasure at her abrupt departure.

Heaven help me. The pompous windbag.

The withdrawing room was mercifully empty, and within a couple of minutes she exited it and walked in the opposite direction from the supper room. A set of French windows at the back of the ballroom led onto the vine-covered terrace that itself was regarded as a public space in which take a breath of fresh air, and as such, her solo presence would not be remarked upon.

* * * *

Nathan lounged against the stone balustrade at the far end of the terrace and waited to see if Evanna would escape the supper room and meet him, although without much optimism. He had glimpsed her throughout the evening, but with a constant stream of admirers clamouring to sign her dance card, and both of her parents in attendance at all other times, he dared not approach her. Each new partner who escorted her to the floor deflated his spirits a little more — other men had the privilege of touching her hand and conversing with her when he himself did not.

Not that he would have found much of an opportunity to do so. His unpopularity with Lord and Lady Kerr did not extend to others in the room. Maybe at any other time he would have been flattered to be so besieged, but no other young lady he was presented to, no matter how pretty, could compare to Evanna.

While walking in the park with her, their conversation had flowed, easily in tune, and he thought—hoped—she was as physically attracted to him as he was to her. A small flash of green caught his eye, and he could not keep the smile from his face as she walked towards him. "Miss Kerr, how delightful to find you here."

She murmured softly, "Papa is in the card room. Mama believes I'm with Mr Percival-Smyth and he thinks I'm in the withdrawing room, so for a few minutes, I can walk with you."

Nathan offered her his arm and the frisson of their physical contact thrilled him as she threaded hers through his. The rear façade of the Macreston mansion had been remodelled in the Palladian style over recent years, and as a wonder of modern architecture it was not untoward for them to view it from the lawn beyond the terrace. He guided Evanna down its stone steps. The summer sun was on the point of sinking below the horizon, but enough light remained for them to admire the ornately carved colonnaded stonework.

The soft hum of conversation drifted on the warm evening air, and Evanna remarked on the musicality of it. "I fall asleep to this happy sound each night, like waves upon the shore. The residence next door to ours must be full of sociable souls."

Knowing full well what was taking place in the house she referred to, Nathan hesitated. "Ah... It is...?"

Evanna glanced sideways, and much as he prayed for it not to happen, he felt the heat of a blush rise on his cheeks.

She narrowed her eyes at him. "You know something, don't you? A disreputable something, I suspect, by the look on your face. Tell me?"

"No. No. I know nothing at all."

His air of assumed innocence didn't fool her for a minute.

"Yes, you do. Tell all, or I shall plague you until you cough it up, you know."

He sidestepped once more. "Cough it up? Where on earth did you hear such an expression? Not exactly ladylike, is it?"

Evanna stuck her nose in the air. "Your diversionary tactics will not work with me, my lord. How about 'spit it out'? Does that suit you better?"

He chuckled. "Hoisted by my own petard, but still, I will neither cough it up nor spit it out. Your father would have my guts for garters if I did."

"Guts for garters!" Evanna giggled, then retorted smugly, "Ah-ha… I have my first clue. Papa would object, but Mama would not. So a disreputable something that is to be kept secret from females in general but not because I'm young and unwed."

"My lips are sealed," he replied, equally smugly.

A female voice cut through the evening air. "Has anyone seen my daughter? I believe she may have lost her way in between the supper room and ballroom."

Evanna disengaged her arm from his and tutted. "Drat it! Your tactic has worked after all, but I shall have it out of you in the end, Nathan McColl. I can be very persistent."

He chuckled. "If it means I will see more of you while you strive to attain your aims, I shall happily encourage you to be so."

She smiled into his eyes. "Until then, I'd best go…and alone."

He watched her trip up the terrace steps.

"I'm here, Mama. The lobster patties were over-rich. I'm afraid I required a little fresh air."

The sun had fallen below the horizon, and Lady Kerr peered into the gloaming—until Evanna added in a *sotto* voice, "Unless you'd have preferred me to offend our hostess by displaying my queasiness to public view?"

Lady Kerr's head swivelled round to face her daughter. "Of course not, but now come along…"

They disappeared from sight, and Nathan smiled into the gathering darkness as he remembered the light-hearted sallies he had just enjoyed. It reassured him to think how Evanna's brown eyes had sparkled with glee as the riposte had flashed back and forth between them—a happy response no other man but himself had managed to evoke so far as he'd seen that evening. She really was the prettiest girl in world.

He longed to kiss her soft lips when she smiled at him, to hold her in his arms, the heat of their bodies pressed close. Her gown was particularly appealing tonight, especially…

Nathan's balls throbbed. He knew his weakness. The temple had taught him that. Feminine curves and ample breasts. He had tried not to let his gaze stray to the scooped neckline of Evanna's dress, but…

Perhaps a visit to the temple was required? Where Celeste's skilled mouth would relieve the pressure? But no. It wasn't her mouth he longed for, but Evanna's. He dragged his thoughts away from the enticing picture before his cock could fully harden. Act Two of the ball beckoned. He would fulfil his obligation as a guest and dance dutifully with the young ladies presented to him, and when Evanna filled his dreams that night, as she surely would, his right hand and imagination would suffice.

Until the day I can make her mine.

Chapter Five

Evanna decided there was something rather dispiriting in being escorted anywhere by Mr Percival-Smyth, but especially to the museum. Somewhere she'd been looking forward to visiting.

At least I have my sisters to help me keep him at arm's length. I can only hope I am able to walk around the exhibits, look my fill and perhaps not exactly ignore him, but give him the lesser part of my attention without giving offence. After all he likes the sound of his own voice so the occasional nod or comment should suffice.

However, once he'd greeted her, oh so properly, his next words infuriated her.

"Now, my dear, some of the exhibits will be beyond your understanding, and although in general I am not in favour of ladies filling their pretty little heads with information not relevant to the role designed for them by Mother Nature..."

He patted her hand in a condescending way she detested and smiled down at her in a manner that made her hand itch.

"You may call on me when you feel overwhelmed, my dear. I will do my best to explain and advise, so long as I deem the subject matter will not prove injurious to your feminine sensibilities, of course."

The only overwhelming thing is your attitude. Your presence, your...your...

The urge to depress the man's pretensions was strong, but how to do so without spoiling her own social standing, which Mr Percival-Smyth could most assuredly accomplish should he take an outright dislike to her? He thought her a demure milk-and-water miss. Perhaps if she disabused him of that particular notion without being openly forthright in her views? She smiled sweetly but injected a tart note into her voice. "I don't doubt you will swiftly correct my alleged assumptions should they not agree with your own, sir. After all, being a *man*, you know best."

His brows knitted together momentarily, but if he'd heard her sarcasm he chose not to acknowledge it, and his expression cleared. "It is most agreeable to me that you recognise that fact."

His initial reaction gave her hope, and Evanna waited while he spoke to his coachman then helped her and her sisters up into his carriage. Their maid he nodded to take a place outside the vehicle on the box before he himself entered and sat on the seat next to Evanna. He left a respectable distance between them, for which Evanna was grateful. Sometimes his pomposity worked in her favour.

Marietta and Catriona chattered away like a pair of magpies about what they wished to see first. Evanna let their conversation wash over her.

"My dear, your sisters are waiting for an answer."

I am not your 'dear'.

"They frequently do."

He frowned. "One of the most graceful qualities of a woman is in her knowing how to listen and answer."

"Ah, but then I have it on good authority I am *only* a young lady, and as these are my sisters, I feel your point is not entirely relevant. After all, I listen and reply to them when *I deem* it necessary." She smiled at him. "Although I do, of course, thank you for reminding me of how *you* think I should go on."

He harrumphed a little at her contradiction, but with her thanking him for his advice, found no more to add. The carriage pulled up at their destination, and he alighted to help her and her sisters out of the vehicle. Maisie jumped down from the box and was ignored until Evanna coughed.

"Marietta, Catriona, walk ahead. I will follow with Maisie at my side…" She paused to look at Mr Percival-Smyth. "While perhaps, you sir, would care lead the way and pause at the exhibits you believe will be of interest to us?"

Her attempt at separating from him did not find favour. "An unwieldy arrangement. Your sisters can be amply chaperoned by the presence your maid, whilst you and I—"

Not likely!

Evanna headed him off quickly. "Mama and Papa only gave permission for this outing on the understanding we would all be in your care at all times."

The look he gave her was strange. Part irritation but tinged with gratification.

"Then let us go in. Stay close, all of you."

Mr Percival-Smyth marched off, his behaviour totally at odds with his words.

Catriona stared after him. "He's not the most amenable of men, is he?"

Satisfied her prospective suitor was becoming less fond by the minute, Evanna smiled inside. However, one fly in the ointment remained, so as she stepped forward to follow him inside she muttered to the twins, "No matter what he says, don't you dare leave me alone with him."

They exchanged a worried glance and nodded.

Evanna would have been the first to own she had yearned to visit the museum, to gaze at paintings and *objets d'art* she had so far only read about, but after an hour she wished she had never voiced her desire to do so within the hearing of Mr Percival-Smyth.

He pontificated, droned on and held forth on everything they saw until Evanna doubted if he ever listened to anything any female said, for presumably he would not have become so wealthy in his business dealings if he treated his male compatriots in the same manner. Eventually she saw her chance to discover if the first part of her surmise was correct when she caught sight of a portrait of Clementine Walkinshaw.

"I can see a bee in a bonnet," she said with a wink to her sisters. "No doubt of Jacobean origin."

Mr Percival-Smyth walked on oblivious, as if she had not spoken. "Now, where next? Hmm… I think we will go this way."

Her veiled reference to the Young Pretender by way of the likeness of his mistress should have provoked some response, she thought. After all, Mr Percival-Smyth's business interests might lie in the Scottish capital, but he hailed from the north of England and was a Sassenach through and through. He had definitely not heard a word she'd said.

Evanna stopped still and spoke louder. "I believe we could use a little refreshment if this establishment possesses a tearoom."

Mr Percival-Smyth halted and turned towards her. She finally had his attention, so glanced over his shoulder in the direction of the sound of chinking china, hoping to spy the opportunity for a few welcome minutes of respite from his presence. "Ah, I see the way. With your leave, come, girls. The private room for the comfort of we ladies is beside it. Perhaps, in our absence, you could secure a table for all of us, sir?"

"I beg your pardon?" His colour rose. "A what?"

"A table. In the tearoom. We will join you as soon as we are able." Her staccato sentences were high-handed, especially when issued by a chit of eighteen to a man of mature years, but Evanna was unrepentant. If he thought her a shrew, so much the better. Without further ado, she turned her back on him and spoke to her sisters, "Follow me. This way."

"Well." Marietta let her breath out in one long *whoosh* as they accessed the ladies withdrawing room. "How on earth can he speak for so long and not draw breath? Evanna, are you seriously thinking of marrying that windbag?"

"I am not," Evanna stated, suspicion dawning. "What makes you think I am?"

The same worried glance as she had seen earlier passed between the twins. "We heard Papa telling Mama you were. He said" — Catriona screwed her eyes up tightly as if to concentrate better — "he said Mr

Percival-Smyth was about to ask for your hand in marriage and by God you'd be glad to agree."

"Glad to? I don't think so."

Marietta continued, "We'd been on our way to the dining room and our parents didn't know we were there, and we couldn't help overhearing. It wasn't eavesdropping, not really. Mama said an older man who doted on you would be more inclined to overlook…" She looked pointedly at Evanna's left hand. "Your…um…you know. Papa agreed and told her, *'it's not a thing that can be hidden forever. She'll give the game away at some point once she's wed. I'm sure Mr Percival-Smyth's maturity will ensure he'll kindly forgive the fault where a younger man will not'*."

"Did he?" Evanna's shoulders slumped. What chance did she have against her parents' determined stance? She had no resources of her own that would enable her to make a life for herself away from Kerr Castle. She counted slowly backwards from ten to gather her thoughts.

There was no point in openly railing at the situation, and however much her parents might nag and insist, neither of them could force the words of acceptance from her mouth against her own will. Stubborn resistance was still her best line of defence, along with her ploy to circumvent Mr Percival-Smyth ever having an opportunity to propose in the first place. She straightened, not wishing to share her disillusionment with the younger girls who still viewed their future prospects through a rosy glow. "We'd best make our way to the tearoom, but I beg of you, whatever Mr Percival-Smyth says or does, act the innocent and give no hint of this conversation. Instead, let us talk of frivolous matters. Of buckles and bows, and puppies and kittens."

"Of frills and furbelows," Catriona giggled.

"He won't get a word in edgeways," Marietta laughed. "We will bore him to death as surely as he has us."

The twins were as good as their word, and Evanna could have kissed them when Mr Percival-Smyth plucked his pocket watch from his waistcoat and said — quite irritably, Evanna thought, "Enjoyable as your company has been, my dears, I believe your parents will be expecting you home."

He laid a golden guinea on the table and clicked his fingers to summon Maisie from the hard-backed chair she was perched upon on the far side of the tearoom by its door. Aware of the plates of dainties that had wafted past Maisie's nose, and the longing glances her maid had made at them, Evanna took her chance to filch a cherry tartlet capped with a crust of burnt sugar from those remaining on the plate and wrap it in her — thankfully unused — hankie.

Her sisters did not cease their chatter during the coach ride home, and Evanna joyfully joined in, bobbing her curtsey once they alighted at Acheson House. "We thank you for the outing, sir. It was most instructive."

Mr Percival-Smyth was not to be so easily dismissed, however, and smiled down on her. "A young lady has so much to learn, and it behoves a gentleman to teach her."

Evanna hid her hand behind her back lest he try to pat it, then her unwanted suitor's departure was once more delayed by the appearance of her papa, who walked out of the front door and beamed.

"Well met, sir. My thanks for entertaining my daughters. I've been out to Musselburgh to see how matters are progressing at the new racecourse. Only from a distance, of course, but it's going to be splendid, eh?"

Percival-Smyth nodded. "Indeed. As one of its capital investors perhaps I could persuade you to accompany me there tomorrow? We shareholders are to discuss the erection of the new grandstand, and as a supporter of the sport, I'm sure your views on the subject would be most welcome."

Lord Kerr's smile almost split his face in two. "It would be both a pleasure and an honour."

Evanna's heart sang.

He will not be at Mrs Murray's picnic, but Nathan will.

She could hardly wait.

* * * *

Nathan hummed — albeit tunelessly — as his valet carefully tied his cravat. Simple but exquisite was the tone of the day, according to Alain. Mrs Murray was one of the racier young matrons. Her picnic would certainly be *nouveaute*, but suitably smart. After careful consideration, he'd settled on a subtle striped waistcoat in shades of grey and silver and a darker grey jacket. One long critical glance in the mirror assured him he was turned out to the nines, and any hostess would deem him a worthy guest.

Alain met him by the front door and whistled. "Very natty."

"I'm not overdressed, am I?" he ventured anxiously. "It's a new activity for me. There's not a lot of suitable picnic weather at home, nor the company for it."

Alain grinned. "Yes, well, the Trossachs cannot boast of the most clement weather, I understand, but you have hit the nail on the head in regard to your attire. Casually subdued in colour but still perfectly turned out. May I presume a certain young lady will also be there?"

Nathan's face heated. He couldn't help it. "She might be."

Alain chuckled. "Well, young cub, I'd like to attempt to take Lady Merrythorpe off your hands if you don't find her so appealing?"

Nathan nodded fervently. "I wish you would. The less eyes looking out for me the better I'll feel."

Alain punched his upper arm. "Faint hearts never won fair lady and all that. Go forth and conquer. And if the conquering doesn't work, I have some brandy that will numb the pain."

Nathan laughed. Alain never failed to raise his spirits. "I'll remember." He picked up his cane and together they sauntered out of the front door.

* * * *

The picnic was in full swing when they were shown through to the garden. Rose-covered arbours, as yet unoccupied, had been set up around the edge of the lawn and dressed with carpeted floors and piles of cushions. On the lawn itself people mingled. Parasols fluttered above the heads of the ladies, gentlemen paid court and liveried servants passed through the crowd bearing trays of sparkling wine.

Nathan spotted Evanna immediately, his gaze irresistibly drawn to her figure and form. Alain scooped up a crystal glass from a passing footman, winked and made his way to Lady Merrythorpe's side. Nathan swallowed hard and drifted, he hoped quite casually, in Evanna's direction. She was standing next to one of the young ladies he'd been obliged to dance with at Lady McCreston's ball. Miss Flora McDavitt giggled at him when he approached.

"Isn't this fun, Lord McColl? We are to gather in informal parties of our own choosing and eat sat on the ground rather than be summoned to the table."

Nathan glanced around. Neither of the Kerr parents were in sight, so he plunged in. "Miss Kerr, would you do me the honour…?"

She threaded her arm through his arm before he'd even finished speaking. "I would be delighted. Shall we stroll and find a spot that's warm but still shady?"

They walked away before Miss Flora could offer to join them, and Nathan chuckled. "Well met, Miss Kerr. Will your parents not object?"

"Papa is not present, thank goodness, and Mama is talking ten to the dozen with her friends. If we slip into an arbour I can escape her for a while."

"A sound plan."

A manservant approached with a tray of brimming goblets. Nathan handed Evanna a glass then took one for himself and nodded his thanks to the man, who bowed and moved off. "I think that if we disappear into the far reaches of it she might not discover us at all," Nathan said with an upward inflection of hope in his voice. "Perfectly above board, of course."

Evanna smiled and sidestepped into the nearest arbour. Nathan placed a cushion on the ground for her to sit on, then took one of his own. She sank down and chinked her glass on his when he followed suit. "This is heavenly. The scent of the blooms is beautiful."

He looked into her eyes. "As are you."

She gazed back. "Lord McColl, are you flirting with me?"

"I think I am, Evanna. Although I've had little practice with the art."

"No more have I, Nathan. But I like it if you are."

"Then I am." His words dried and he took a gulp of his wine. "What am I meant to say next?"

She giggled and sipped her own. "That I'm a wonder, or a goddess, or some such thing."

Nathan's cheeks heated. He couldn't prevent it. *Oh, Lord! Of all the words, did it have to be that one?*

Evanna laughed louder and teased, "So, by the look on your face, the house next door and what...? Goddess? Wonderful goddess?"

He spluttered. "No. Of course not…"

She looked down at her knees and wrapped her arms around her middle region while her shoulders shook.

"Evanna, I'm sorry if that sounded uncomplimentary to yourself. I…I…didn't mean to insinuate you aren't wonderful."

She looked up at him, her eyes sparkling with mirth as tears ran down her cheeks. "Nathan McColl, is the residence next door to our lodgings a house of ill repute?"

That he had not upset her by his inability to turn a compliment was a relief, but still left him fumbling words. "Um… Well…"

She wiped her eyes on the back of her hand then drank another mouthful of wine. "I told you I'd have it out of you, so come on, spit it out. I promise I'm not cross or shocked, just rather curious. I take it you've been inside?"

"Ah, well…Alain took me."

"And?"

He crossed his fingers and fibbed a little. "It's all rather respectable really. No drunkenness or lewdness. An elderly lady plays the pianoforte and people sit around chatting like they would at any other party…"

"But?"

"If two people like each other enough then…um… they slip out of the room for one more private."

Evanna giggled. "How do the, ah…female entertainers come and go? I've not seen any more than mundane activity from the street."

Her high spirits were infectious, and Nathan grinned. "The guests enter the residence in the normal manner, albeit discreetly, after dark. Their entertainment, as you so politely put it, by way of the garden at the back of the house."

"The garden? What fun. Hmm… We have no evening engagement tonight and it will be warm enough for a stroll."

The gleam in her eye brought Nathan up short. What had he done? If he had guessed her intention correctly, Evanna might be mistaken for one of the ladies of the night and be propositioned.

No!

"Evanna, you daren't. It's not to be thought of."

She only laughed. "A dare, is it? Well, I shall prove to you I am not so lily-livered. I can and I will."

For all her merriment, he could tell that she meant it. There was only one thing to be done. "Not alone. I will accompany you."

"You will? How wonderful. It will be an adventure. It's naughty I know, but I so wish to take a peek. There is wicker gate at the rear of our garden. I will meet you there once it is fully dark." Her dimple appeared and she added cheekily, "If you yourself dare."

Footsteps approached as Nathan opened his mouth to protest. A rather effete young man bowed deeply.

"Miss... *Madamooselle*, your hostess engaged my services for the entertainment of her guests. *Je suis* create your likeness? Such a gracious profile, I fear I may not do it or your beauty justice."

Evanna looked startled at the intrusion then inclined her head. "I suppose so."

The artist clapped his hands together. "*Bon. Permit moi to regardez* you for a moment..."

He tilted his head to one side in what Nathan considered a parody of deep thought. "*Oui.* Perfection. *M'sieur*, dinna agree with me? Is she no a wee...ah, exceptional?"

Nathan suppressed a smile at the way the man's accent varied from pseudo-French to thick Glaswegian and replied gravely, "All of that. I will be interested to see the result of...?"

"A silhouette, *M'sieur*." The artiste kissed his fingers. "It will be exquisite." He delved into a cloth satchel and produced a sheet of black paper along with a pair of scissors. "*Alors, je* create a wee gem."

Evanna's lips twitched, and Nathan held back his laugh. He had to ask the man's name. "I wonder, sir, will you share you name so I can say who created such a masterpiece?"

The man gave him a quizzical glance and chuckled. "*M'sieur* George."

Nathan grinned. "Dod for short?"

M'sieur George shrugged. "Ock, aye. Ahm dein ma best tae lose the weegie. Everyone wants a Frenchie emigre these days. Not so much work for a native-born Glaswegian, no matter what the talent."

Scottish to his core, Nathan had no problem with the vernacular. Dod, a nickname for George, was a weegie, a man who hailed from the city of Glasgow. The artist snipped away then sighed happily. "That'll dae…"

M'sieur George handed the result of his scissor work to Nathan. He stared at Evanna's head and shoulders in profile, a perfect outline of her no more than three inches high created in mere minutes. "It will more than do. You have quite some talent, Dod. Look, Ev—" He caught himself just in time. "Miss Kerr."

Evanna smiled at the small piece of black card. "I think it is, my lord."

Nathan dug into his pocket, pulled out a silver half-a-crown and handed it to *M'sieur* George. "We shall certainly pass your name along and recommend your work." The artist accepted the coin with a bow then walked away with mincing steps. Evanna caught Nathan's eye, and as they exchanged a merry glance at the playacting antics of the braw Scotsman, they were interrupted once more.

"There you are. I wondered where you'd got to." Miss Flora waltzed into the arbour, plonked herself down on a cushion without so much as a by your leave and gazed at *M'sieur's* retreating back. "Who was that?"

"A travelling artist," Nathan informed their uninvited guest a touch stiffly as he placed the silhouette carefully into an inside pocket—and not a minute too soon.

"Evanna. Evanna. I best not find you alone with—"

"Good day, Lady Kerr." Miss Flora smiled sunnily. "This picnic is delightful, don't you think?"

Much as he had been cursing the unexpected arrival of Miss Flora, Nathan now blessed her for it as Lady Kerr's expression changed from crossly haughty to huffily discontent at the sight of there being a group of three sitting in the arbour. "I can't say it's to my taste. Far too frivolously informal. No one knows where anyone else is at any given time. Come, Evanna. I have called for our carriage. We are departing."

"Oh, Mama. Must we?" Evanna protested.

"Yes, we must," Lady Kerr stated in a voice that brooked no argument, before spearing Miss Flora with her glare. "And you, young lady, come with me. I will restore you to your mother before we leave. Good day to you, my lord."

Both girls jumped to their feet as Lady Kerr swept around. Evanna managed to mouth "tonight" at him as they curtsied their farewells before they followed on. He smiled, his thoughts a jumbled contradiction of anticipation overlaid with an equal measure of trepidation for the potential of their madcap assignation to go woefully astray. Her eagle-eyed parent might prevent her from leaving the house and meeting him at all—but he would not think it. He would be at the appointed place well ahead of time.

Chapter Six

Evanna hummed happily as she prepared for the evening. Dinner was to be taken informally, *en famille*, and after her maid's appreciation of the cherry tartlet, she felt entirely comfortable to quiz Maisie gently about what she most needed to know. What would she find if she stepped outside the boundary of the garden?

On her return from the museum, she had run upstairs and unwrapped the pastry concealed within her hankie. The thick sugar crust had done its job — it was still perfectly round and there had been no leakage of fruit jam. Maisie's eyes widened when Evanna presented her with the small, sweet pie.

"It's a' fae me? Ye ken I've longed to take a taste o' the dainties when I carry the plate in for afternoon tea but Cook gives those returned to the kitchen no eaten ta the upper servants, no' we lower maids or the houseboy."

"Then you must eat it at once, this minute, Maisie. This treat is for you. I will not see it confiscated by any of the upper staff for your taking it down to the kitchen to eat."

Maisie's eyes closed, her expression blissful as she bit, chewed and swallowed. Evanna smiled. That such a small thing could give such pleasure. Two blobs of sticky red jam had stained the otherwise pristine white linen hankie when she was done. Maisie dabbed them with a wetted fingertip. "I'll launder it immediately, miss. It'll be as good as new."

"You must question my skill with a pastry fork should you be spotted doing so," Evanna laughed.

Maisie giggled and ran downstairs with it then, as she'd promised, returned the hankie in spotless condition come the morning.

Evanna surveyed her gowns. She wanted to appear beautiful to Nathan's eyes but one of Madame Coeur's creations would raise eyebrows when dining at home with no guests present. Of the gowns she had bought with her, one of royal blue satin caught her eye. Plainly fashioned with no frills or ruffles, the sheen of the material was sumptuous, and it fastened at the front with small silver buttons. If all went well with her plan to creep out and meet Nathan later, she wouldn't require the services of her maid when she returned home.

Maisie certainly approved of the dress once Evanna put it on. "It's lovely, miss. I've always thought you look braw and bonny in it. See how it shines when it catches the light!"

Evanna popped the last button through its hole, happy to return the warm glow she experienced at the compliment with a favour she could freely grant by her own say so. "As you can see, I'll need no assistance to disrobe later tonight, so you may take the rest of the evening for yourself, Maisie."

"You are kind, miss. If thae's anything else…?"

Evanna drifted to the window. "I sometimes wonder what lies beyond the garden gate? The shrubs and greenery are in the way. I can't make it out."

"It's no much. A ginnel between the houses on our street and the ones in the street behind, so's deliveries and the like can be made ta tha back door. Halfway along is the common well for our houseboy to draw fresh water for the household, and up the far end is where we empties the pots into the communal…um…"

"Cesspit?" Evanna guessed.

"Aye," Maisie confirmed. "The cludgie. It ain't too bad, though. There's a wooden cover so it dinnae smell too ripe, and the night soil cart comes twice a week."

"And the servants use they alley to come and go, do they? It must be a busy place."

Maisie grinned. "Plenty of coming and going. We maids do like to have a bit of a lark out back while we're about our work." She put her hand in front of her mouth. "I should'na have said that. If Mrs McHarg finds out, I'll be right in the mire."

"She won't find out from me," Evanna reassured her.

"I'm nae a tittle-tattle either, miss," Maisie stated stoutly.

Evanna smiled. She and her maid were in perfect accord. Confidences had been exchanged. Trust was established. What one knew about the other would not be revealed. "Enjoy your free time, Maisie. I'll see you come the morn."

Maisie's grin lit her face. "That I will. Goodnight and bless you, miss."

Her maid practically skipped from the room.

Evanna followed her out and descended the stairs at a more sedate place to find dinner was, as she'd half-expected, a purely feminine affair, as her Papa had not yet returned from Musselburgh. By nine of the clock, Evanna was wishing herself anywhere else bar the dining table as Mama opined on Mr Percival-Smyth's perceived attributes. Catriona and Marietta stared at their plates, pink-cheeked but not daring to give voice to their views, while Evanna held her tongue, deeming it hopeless to contradict her mother's glowing compliments on the man.

She covered her yawn with her hand as the timepiece chimed ten. "You must excuse me, Mama. The excitement of our trip to the museum has fair worn me out."

Catriona and Marietta looked nothing but relieved at her intervention and said in unison, "And us, Mama. We are so fatigued."

Lady Kerr did not look best pleased and huffed. "Well, I was looking forward to discussing bridesmaids and posies, and of course plaids to tie the knot, but I suppose…if you must."

Evanna could bear it no longer and jumped to her feet. "Mama, I'm sorry, but I must. Another time perhaps… Goodnight."

She curtsied in a dutiful manner, watched her sisters do the same, and made her way thankfully out of the room, followed by Catriona and Marietta.

"Phew." Marietta waved her hand in front of her face. "Mama is going full-on with marriage ideas, isn't she? I do not envy you, Evanna. We all know what she is like when she gets the bit between her teeth."

Evanna nodded gloomily. They did.

The solitude of her room had never been more welcome, and as ever, she opened her window wide after she'd shut her bedroom door behind her. A tingle of excitement ran down her spine when she heard the notes of a pianoforte float through it. Perhaps, just perhaps, Nathan might try to steal a kiss from her tonight. She looked forward to him doing so very much!

A clatter sounded beyond the door and made her start. Papa must have returned. The house quietened as she gazed into the garden, the moon visible in the night sky. She had endured all her mother had had to say, it was time to escape. Evanna crept to the door, opened it a crack and listened. Silence.

The soft calfskin soles of her slippered feet made barely a sound as she crept stealthily back down the stairs and the candles in their wall sconces guttered, but still lit the shadowy corridors. The dining room, so recently hostile, was now blessedly empty of anyone but herself, and she made her way into the garden by way of its French doors.

The moon was full enough to ensure she did not stumble once outside, and her breath hissed triumphantly through her teeth as she unlatched the wicker gate. Honeysuckle and jasmine hit her nose as she stepped through — planted by some cany gardener to mask any bad odour escaping the cesspit, she guessed. She peered left then right, and a shadow detached itself from a nearby bush.

"Evanna? You came?"

Her heart leapt and she giggled once she realised — with some relief — who it was. "Did you doubt me, my lord? I told you I would."

"My lord?" he said with a smile in his voice. "Is that anyway to address your fellow adventurer in this daring escapade?"

She laughed at his like-minded funning tone. "Nathan McColl, you are as outrageous as me."

The pitter-patter of heeled shoes tapped on the hard-tamped earth of the track. Nathan twitched something from his pocket, thrust it at her, and put his finger on his lips. "Shhh — no names in earshot of any other. Put this on."

Evanna felt soft cloth in her hand. The velvet of an opera mask. She fastened it around the back of head just as a cloaked figure smelling of lily of the valley wafted past and muttered, "The door you need is round the front, sir. Streetside. Number eleven."

Evanna clutched Nathan's arm as she disappeared. "Was she one of the godd — ?"

"Yes, she was," he confirmed, answering her question before she completed it.

Giggles tickled her belly. "And we can go inside? Both of us?"

"No, you cannot. That wasn't part of the dare."

Another sweet-smelling, cloaked female fluttered past. "Gentlemen and their lady guests enter the Temple by way of the street door, sir. Number eleven."

Evanna's high spirits bubbled up and out. "It is now."

"Evanna... No!"

She darted to the side of him. "I shall knock at the front door and ask to be admitted."

He caught her arm. "Not without me, you won't."

She smiled and slipped her hand in his, the thrill of touching his skin tingling down her spine. "Tell me how to go on and I'll behave, I promise. I just want to take a peek."

His hand closed around her own. "When we enter the Temple do not remove your mask. Look without making eye contact with those in the room. Converse solely with me."

The alley was not so narrow that they couldn't walk side by side. Nathan guided her steps to the far end of the ginnel, and they stepped out onto the paved surface of the street.

* * * *

The proprietress inclined her head in a small nod of recognition to him when they were admitted into the vestibule of the Temple. A silver half-crown secured the required ticket, and he slipped his arm possessively around Evanna's waist as he led her into the salon. She did not object and moved even closer, matching her footsteps with his. Her eyes widened at the tableau that met her gaze and she whispered, "Oh, my. They're not wearing much, are they? I feel somewhat overdressed."

A love seat at the side of the salon offered a perfect but discreet view of the proceedings and he walked towards it with a grin. "Is it not what you were expecting? We can sit here and listen to the music for a while if you'd like?"

She sat with aplomb and giggled. "I don't know what I was expecting, really. Perhaps I should have come out dressed in just my petticoat."

"To have done so would mark you as a lady available for company," he chuckled.

Her eyes sparkled with mirth as a male guest gave a diaphanously clad buttock a squeeze as a couple made their way through the archway that led to the intimate chambers. A footman approached and offered Nathan a glass of wine from his tray. He took one and gave it to Evanna before taking one for himself.

The pianist was playing the best approximation of the *Overture to the Magic Flute* that could be managed with only one pair of hands and a single instrument. Evanna's foot tapped her foot in time to the tune while her gaze darted here and there around the salon.

Nathan looked only at Evanna. There was no other female in the room who could compare so far as he was concerned, and whether he should or no, he was making the most of his opportunity to feast his eyes on the deep cleft between her breasts and imagine their full roundness filling his hands. His cock twitched as he tried to picture her nipples. Were they pink or brown? How would they respond to the touch of his mouth? A delicious thought. His shaft began to harden. He was brought from his reverie with a sudden guilty start as Evanna gasped, "Oh, goodness!"

Thankfully, it was not his burgeoning groin she was staring at, but the door leading into the salon from the entrance vestibule. He glanced over his shoulder and saw a female who, despite her face covering, he immediately recognised as Lady Merrythorpe, and beside her, the unmistakable figure of Alain.

Damn!

Alain wouldn't let the cat out of the bag if he recognised Evanna beneath her opera mask, that he was confident of, but what Lady Merrythorpe's reaction might be he was not so sure. Was she the type of woman likely to confide in a close friend or two that she had visited the Temple? He didn't know her well enough to answer the question, but if it were the case and Evanna's name was mentioned, he was sure such a delicious *on dit* would be passed on. Arbitrary as it might be, as a married woman, Lady Merrythorpe's reputation would suffer no lasting harm, whereas unwed Evanna's would be sunk beyond repair.

Action was needed. Evanna must be whisked out of sight. He jumped to his feet and stood in front of her, shielding her from their view. Lady Merrythorpe and Alain were blocking the route out of the Temple, leaving the archway as the only alternative avenue by which to disappear from the room. He took Evanna's hand. "Stand in front of me and walk through the arch to the private chambers. We can hide in one until they quit the salon."

"How will we know when they've gone?"

"It is not untoward for me to be in the Temple, only you. I will return at intervals and peruse the salon. I don't suppose they will linger for long."

Evanna giggled. "Nor I. Wine and song is hardly the activity they are here to enjoy, is it?"

Their compromising situation successfully avoided, Nathan relaxed sufficiently to chuckle. "They'll be in the salon for no longer than it takes to sip a glass of wine." He guided Evanna out of the salon and up the stairs into a hallway lined with closed doors. Lit lanterns stood on the floor before some, marking the private boudoir beyond the door as unoccupied. Nathan scooped up the first lit lamp he came to and opened the door. "You can remove your mask in here."

Evanna did so. He followed suit then she preceded him in and looked around her with bright-eyed interest as the golden glow illuminated the interior. "It's quite ordinary, then? A bed, a washstand, a…" The oddly configured stool caught her attention. "Except this is strangely shaped."

The spanking stool, as Nathan now knew it was called, was employed for more than the administration of rod and paddle for those whose pleasure was heightened by a touch of pain, and he couldn't help his thoughts straying that way—Evanna bent over the stool, her pert rear and glistening channel displayed for his pleasure as she awaited the entry of his cock.

Mmm…

She regarded him as if awaiting an explanation. He blushed, chose not to enlighten her, and merely shrugged. She accepted his gesture as a reply that he didn't know either and instead remarked on his pink face. "It's very warm in here, isn't it? Remove your jacket, if you like. I don't mind."

That he was feeling over-warm for other reasons he also kept to himself, but his jacket he gratefully dispensed with, along with his waistcoat. Evanna wandered over to the bed, sat on the side of it and wiggled her rear. "The mattress is very well stuffed." Then she began to bounce.

Oh, God!

Her breasts swayed to the motion, the full moons of their plumpness rising and falling above the scooped neckline of her gown. Nathan swallowed hard and tugged at his cravat.

She patted the space beside her and laughed. "Come and try. It's fun."

He held his nerve and joined her, then grinned. She was right. He bumped up and down, using his heavier weight so she bounced higher until she collapsed backward, helpless with giggles. He reclined on his side and waited for them to subside.

Evanna looked into his eyes once she'd caught her breath. "I've never been kissed, you know."

Her tone was conversational. The look in her eyes was not. He leant over her and accepted the invitation they offered. She parted her lips when their mouths touched, allowing his tongue to entwine with hers, a sensation so heavenly Nathan never wanted it to end, and no more it seemed, did Evanna. She threaded her fingers through the back of his hair, her mouth demanding more, her breasts pressing against his chest, and when their mouths parted he continued to press small kisses onto the soft skin under her ear and down her neck.

His cravat, already loosened, unravelled to the plucking of her fingers, and she slipped her hand inside his shirt and explored the curls of hair on his chest. The buttons on her bodice popped open at his touch, leaving the longed-for sight of her nipples on view. Standing proud, two luscious strawberries begging for his attention. He fastened his mouth over one then the other, the generous orbs of the flesh beneath them spilling through his fingers as he squeezed. Evanna writhed. "Oh, Nathan… Yes…"

A line had been crossed and there was no turning back then, for either of them. He had touched Evanna intimately, and she had welcomed him doing so. Desire overwhelmed his senses and coherent thought fled when she reached down and traced the outline of his erection over the material of his breeches. He pushed her skirts up over her thighs and stroked between her legs. She was wet. Oh so wet. Ready to receive his cock. He freed it, eased the head of his shaft inside her and met a moment of resistance.

Her maidenhead?

In the throes of imminent ecstasy it mattered not when Evanna moaned softly and pushed her pelvis against his, encouraging him on. Riding his passion he thrust deeper and faster until her back arched, bucking up and away from the mattress. She wrapped her legs around his thighs with a triumphant, "Yes! Yes!"

His own climax exploded.

"My beautiful, Evanna. I love you so much."

"I love you too…"

Breathing hard, he disengaged and rolled onto his side, put his arms around her and held her tight. "My love, I shall call on your father in the morning and write to my own. We may have to wait a little while to call the banns. I'm sure His Grace will express his delight by return, but he likes to travel in style. It will take him a week or two after the receipt of our news for him to reach us."

She stroked down the side of his face. "How I wish I could offer you the same reassurance in the manner of my parents' reply."

With the crux of the matter that had been perplexing him finally voiced, their newfound intimacy emboldened Nathan to ask, "Why, though? I don't wish to blow my own trumpet, but to turn down a viscount, the heir to a dukedom, seems rather odd."

Evanna sighed. "I didn't realise until we left the familiarity of life at Kerr Castle and came to Edinburgh, that my parents hold differing views to myself on what constitutes my future happiness. Some might call their outlook practical, but to me, cynical is a more appropriate word. You are dependent on your father's goodwill for your maintenance, and to be blunt, I have another suitor rich enough to earn their preferment."

Nathan's heart sank. "Mr Percival-Smyth?"

A tear rolled down Evanna's cheek. "The man is not my preferred anything. I do all I can to resist his overtures but he is persistent and encouraged to be so. I cannot vouch for your reception if you seek an interview with my father tomorrow."

Nathan had heard enough. It was time to step forward and be a man. "No! I love you and you me, and we must thwart your parents' schemes. Meet me tomorrow night at the same time? I will have a carriage waiting. We can drive through the night and put some miles between us and Edinburgh, then find a kirk come the daylight. This is Scotland and we are both over sixteen. Once our vows have been spoken and registered by the minister, they cannot be undone. Once we are wed we can move forward and forge a life together."

"Oh, Nathan… Do we dare?"

He wiped her tear away with the pad of his thumb and kissed her. "For you, I would. Will you?"

She kissed him back. "Yes. I would dare anything for you."

* * * *

Evanna stole silently back into the house, feeling as if she were walking on air. She was a woman now, not a girl. In less than two days she would be Nathan's bride and wife. She had received somewhat of a surprise to glimpse Percival-Smyth as she and Nathan made their way out of the Temple, but thankfully he had not recognised her, and the dratted man wouldn't be a threat or a worry to her peace of mind for much longer. She hugged the secret to her after she'd undressed and climbed into bed. Nathan was right.

They both knew their own minds. Escape from parental control was the only way to achieve the happiness they both desired, but she would have to be careful not to betray her excitement. One more day, then she and Nathan would be together for the rest of their lives.

So late had she returned home it seemed that no sooner had she closed her eyes than Maisie was in her bedroom heralding the start of a new day. The last day before her new life began. Her hands trembled a little — nerves overlaid with anticipation for night to arrive once more. In the interests of regaining the composure required before coming face to face with her parents, Evanna decided to forgo breakfast.

"I'm not particularly hungry, Maisie. I'll linger here for now and come downstairs later."

Her respite did not last long as Maisie returned not even an hour later.

"I've been sent to fetch you, miss. Your father and lady mother want to see you in his study. I said as you weren't even dressed yet, an' they said you was to do so without delay. Bit fidgety, the pair of 'em, if you was to ask me."

The words 'without delay' and 'fidgety' did nothing to soothe Evanna's nerves. Could Nathan have changed their plan and sought an interview with Papa while she'd been out of earshot upstairs? "Ah… Have there been any visitors this morning?"

"No, miss. Not unless you count the houseboy what bought a letter. Mind, their receiving it seemed to be what set 'em off."

Oh, goodness! Nathan, have you set out your proposal in writing?

Evanna's knees wobbled as she put her feet to the floor, and she was glad of her maid's assistance as she fumbled all fingers and thumbs while she dressed — even forgetting herself for a moment and reaching for her stocking with her left hand.

Her father was sat behind his desk with her mother at his side when she entered the study. Papa waved her towards the vacant seat in front of it. "Sit."

She did so and clasped her shaking hands together, her heart beating furiously — but instead of beginning the homily she believed she was to receive, her mother smiled. A broad smile. A happy smile. A smile that filled Evanna with foreboding. "As you know, Papa accompanied Mr Percival-Smyth to Musselburgh yesterday, and you will wish to thank him for it, for his doing so has done the trick."

Her father acknowledged Mama's salutation with a smile of his own, although his expression was more smug than happy. He nodded at a sheet of vellum laid on the desk. "He must have worked like the wind to have had this prepared in such short order, and I compliment him for it. No shilly-shallying. A man of action, who even though obviously smitten, remains clear-headed in matters of business."

Even upside down, the curly letters of the opening lines of script written upon it were legible…

Marriage Contract
The marriage agreement between Mr Wilbur Percival-Smyth, (the First Party) and Miss Evanna Kerr (the Second Party) (collectively, the Parties)
The Parties are to be married…

Evanna's stomach churned. She opened her mouth to object but Mama, as if predicting she would do so, interjected quickly, "Wait until you hear the terms, Evanna. Through your father's good offices, they are generous. Very generous indeed."

Papa rubbed his hands together, his voice holding more than hint of triumphant glee. "They certainly are. I did not expect even half of my demands to be met, but they have been, and more besides." He cleared his throat. "So, in the matter of your dowry, he waives all entitlement. For your sisters, he will settle a thousand pounds on each of them on the day they themselves marry…"

Mama clapped her hands together. "Did you hear that, Evanna? Not only we will *not* have to pay your dowry, but Mr Percival-Smyth will provide one for each of the younger girls…"

Papa tutted at her mother's interruption and continued, "For your household expenses five hundred pounds per quarter will be settled without question, although very sensibly I must say, sums above this amount must be brought to his attention beforehand for his consideration and approval. In the matter of your personal allowance, one hundred pounds per quarter will be paid into an account for your own use."

Mama pulled a hankie from her pocket and dabbed her eyes. "You will never have to fret over whether you may spend a shilling or two. I am so happy for you."

Evanna sat straighter. "No. I have no liking for the man."

Mama gasped. "What do mean, no liking? Think on it, child. This is just the start. Keep him sweet and he will dote on you more and more. Anything you desire will be within your reach."

Evanna squared her shoulders and stated firmly, "No. Not for all the riches in the world would I wish to be married to Mr Percival-Smyth."

Papa scowled and thumped the desk. "And never in the world did I imagine a child of mine would show such ingratitude for the efforts her parents have expended on her behalf. Return to your room at once! You will reconsider your position, along with the fact your younger sisters' future happiness hangs on your decision too."

Evanna fled. Thanks goodness her and Nathan's plans were already in place. She would hide in her room until the time was right. Maisie could bring her luncheon on a tray. Only her maid never appeared, and when Evanna thought to run down to the kitchen to request some bread and soup, she found her bedroom door was locked.

Despondency didn't set in until the afternoon when, with a releasing *click*, her mama walked into the room bearing a jug of water and a hunk of bread. She set them down on the night table beside Evanna's bed. "You will think it harsh, I dare say, but what I do is for your own good. You have been given a wonderful offer and the family fortunes rely on you accepting it. You are young and dream of love, but take it from me, it does not last. A life of ease is preferable. When you come to your senses we will speak again. Until then…" She waved a hand at the meagre sustenance, walked away, and the lock clicked once more.

Evanna ate the bread, drank the water and waited by her open window as the sun set. Nathan would appear. She was sure of it. She would call out and relay what had happened.

* * * *

She was still waiting come the morning, and from there, the worse weeks of her life began.

Maisie was finally permitted to bring her meagre rations after four days. Evanna passed her a folded note she had prepared, but two days later Maisie muttered the news—she had been unable to deliver it. Viscount McColl had left Edinburgh and returned to his estate in the Trossachs.

It took two weeks of near starvation for Evanna to accede. Weak from hunger, and without hope of rescue, she signed her name to the marriage contract then, as listless as a rag doll, she mouthed her wedding vows. The consummation of the matter providing the final nail in the coffin.

* * * *

Mr Percival-Smyth—she would never be able to call him Wilbur—patted her hand. "You are overawed and nervous, your parents have given me to understand, but the moment has come for you to oblige your husband as he claims his conjugal rights. Lay on the bed, my dear. Spread your legs and I will do the rest."

Evanna felt nauseous at the thought but complied. He shrugged off his belted dressing gown, strutted nearer, plucked at the hem of her nightgown and pushed it up over her thighs. "Oh, yes…let me see what I've paid for. A sweet little muff that will feel the spear of my manhood shortly…"

His fingers jabbed and probed between her legs before he pushed her nightgown higher. "Two fat titties… Very nice." He tugged and twisted her nipple.

Evanna gasped at his rough handling of her and attempted to wriggle out of his grasp, but he mistook her response for a sign of encouragement. "Oh, you like that, do you?"

He bent his head and bit. Evanna squealed, which only seemed to excite him more. His semi-flaccid shaft fully hardened. He mounted her and pushed his cock into her channel, then kneaded her breasts with his hands as he began to move. Evanna tensed at his unwelcome intrusion, but he did not notice as he thrust and thrust and took his pleasure. He climaxed silently, rolled to his side breathing heavily, and patted her shoulder. "You stir my loins to action like no woman has for years with your luscious body and demure ways. Innocent as you are, you have no notion of a man's carnal desires, but you will grow accustomed to a wife's duty to submit to her husband's need for coitus."

He reached out and rolled the nub of her nipple between his thumb and forefinger. It puckered, not in pleasure but in distress at the clumsiness of his touch. He eyed her chest greedily. "These, I like. Henceforth, when I address you with the words, 'Madam, we have a private matter to discuss', you will excuse yourself from whatever activity is occupying your time and come to this bedroom. When I enter it…" Evanna pressed her knees together as his gaze roamed down her body and rested on the triangle between her legs. "I expect to find you naked, laid upon the bed, ready for my delectation."

She felt sick to the bottom of her stomach and turned her face away, but the floodgates opened when he clambered out of bed and looked at the sheet. "Your maidenhead. I see no sign of it…?"

The somnolent cloud of apathy lifted, and in its place a mist descended — its colour as red as the stain he had expected to see on the bedsheet. How dare Percival-Smyth prod, poke and invade her body as if it were his God-given right? Boiling anger raced through her veins at the brutish act of intercourse to which she had been subjected and his presumption of ownership that he believed excused his behaviour, and at her parents for their coercion in bringing her to this point, and at herself, for succumbing to their manipulation.

She sat up, adjusted her nightgown to cover her exposed skin, and every ounce of disgusted loathing roiling through her poured out in her voice. "If your requirement was for a *virgin*, sir, you should have set it out in the marriage contract. In all good conscience, my parents would not then have *insisted* I append my name to the document."

His brow furrowed at first, as if he were struggling to comprehend the alteration in her previously meek demeanour — then he faced her, his expression ominously cold as the import of her words sunk in. "You are declaring to me that before this night you were not pure? That another man has touched your flesh before me?"

Evanna spat her defiance. "You've taken what you wanted. What does it matter?"

His expression darkened. "I beg your pardon?"

"So you should. My body is my own, not yours to command according to your own selfish desires." A snatch of conversation overhead at the Temple came to mind.

The sanctimonious toad!

She threw his words back at him, "Perhaps you should apply to my parents for a *refund,* sir, if the goods *paid* for are not to your satisfaction."

Percival-Smyth's face turned puce. He grabbed her arm, dragged her from the bed and pushed her to the floor. "Such wickedly wanton talk as I never thought to hear! By your words you condemn yourself guilty of an act of common copulation. Repent at once! Kneel at my feet and beg my forgiveness."

Partially winded, Evanna retorted through gritted teeth, "I will never apologise, nor beg forgiveness, for an act of love freely given and received."

He picked up his robe and put it on, but removed the belt of it. "I have offered you a chance of redemption, madam. You leave me no choice but to declare you a woman of abhorrent morals. According to the rule of law there is only one punishment for the likes of you…"

Chapter Seven

Now

As ever, what had followed, Evanna's mind shied away from. Memories too painful to remember, she willfully diverted her thoughts by determinedly finishing her sherry and donning a clean nightgown that had never been within sight of a man. She would read for a while before retiring to bed, but as she reached for a book of poems, a commotion sounded on the street beneath her window. She opened it wide, and an acrid smell hit her nose. Men were running towards a glow in the distance. "Fire! Fire! At the Armstrong house…"

Evanna's silent scream echoed inside her head. *Nathan!*

Was he still inside? George would have surely offered him some form of refreshment after their long journey, even if it was only a large brandy to get over

Gordon's shocking outburst. She flung a pelisse over her nightgown and ran.

* * * *

Before

Who would have thought it? That their madcap escapade to the Temple could lead to this bed in the boudoir and the consummation of their love. Nathan hugged Evanna close to his chest and smiled. *My future wife. My love.* His father would be delighted with his choice of bride, he was sure. His Grace might have wished his son to have a season or two in London — it was *de rigueur* for the aristocracy to gain a little town polish — but an English alliance had never been on the cards for the heir of the Duke of Glenard.

Loyal Scots all knew who the rightful king should be, and it wasn't the Hanoverian interloper who currently sat on the throne. These sentiments were, of course, never expressed in public, the reach of the palace was long, but at private dinners the toast 'to the prince over the water' was made by loyal Scots, and the Kerrs were Scottish through and through.

Evanna stirred. "The servants rise early. I should return home before my absence is discovered."

Nathan kissed the top of her head, then her lips and released her from his arms. She shook her skirts to cover her naked lower limbs, buttoned her bodice and blushed as she noticed the mark they had made on the sheet. He looked at a flask of rose-coloured oil standing on the washstand, rearranged his own clothing and fetched it. A little of the contents dripped upon the sheet dispersed the stain and — an accidental spillage of sensual oil was all that was left behind. They smirked at each other, then Nathan replaced his mask. "I'll check if the coast is clear."

The main salon was thankfully empty of even the pianist, so he sped back to Evanna and beckoned her forward. She took his arm and they walked down the corridor. A cough and a husky laugh from someone behind brought them up short. Nathan pulled Evanna into a close embrace to hide her face as a couple walked by. The profile of the man showed clearly into dim light of a flickering sconce and if he was not mistaken — and he was certain he was not — it was his rival, Mr Percival-Smyth, accompanied by the goddess Celeste.

"You'll have your work cut out on that front, sir. Madam doesn't issue refunds."

"I don't see why I should have to pay if you can't do your job properly."

"Except it wasn't me that wasn't up to the job was it, sir?"

Evanna gasped at the sound of Mr Percival-Smyth's voice then giggled into Nathan's chest as they listened to the exchange. "Did that mean what I think it does?"

He chuckled. "It certainly sounded as if he couldn't rise to the occasion!"

She snorted. "How two-faced is he? Prosy, bumptious and oh so prudish on the one side and visiting ladies of the night on the other!"

They exchanged a grin and, with the corridor once more deserted, made their way out of the Temple.

The sky was beginning to lighten to summer's early dawn as they stepped out onto the street, and they hastened to the ginnel for one last lingering kiss with the whispered promise of "until tonight" before Evanna left him at the wicker gate.

Nathan walked back to his godfather's house, his mind alive with plans. There was a lot to be arranged, but nothing could be done until the city was awake. His bed beckoned. A few hours of sleep would fit him for the task.

* * * *

Alain was as late down to breakfast as he. Nathan sat to table with a plate of ham and eggs. Alain slouched in his seat and ordered a beefsteak to be served rare, accompanied by a large tankard of claret. He regarded his plate blearily when it was set before him and chugged a large mouthful of wine. "Hell's bells, Lady Merrythorpe is demanding. You can have her back if you like. Your stamina maybe better than mine."

Nathan chuckled and tucked into his portion with an excellent appetite. "I thank you, but no. I find myself very well suited elsewhere. I am minded to take a little excursion. Do you have a livery hire you would care to recommend?"

Thankfully, Alain did not enquire as to where he was headed but answered wearily, "Benson's beside the castle wall have a fair reputation for treating their beasts well. For myself, as soon as I've filled my belly and am duly fortified, I'm returning upstairs for another forty winks."

Nathan grinned, finished his meal then sauntered towards the castle. An hour later a suitable equipage had been hired, with a boy engaged to drive the carriage and pair to the entrance to the ginnel and hold their heads until they were needed. On his return to his godfather's house he packed a small valise with the bare essentials he required for a short absence after deciding, for discretion's sake, not to confide in Alain. A letter explaining matters could be dispatched express once he and Evanna had taken their vows at the kirk.

* * * *

Excitement raced through his veins as darkness fell. He arrived at the ginnel and loitered in the cover of a large lavender bush. An hour later he began to pace, but he didn't leave his post until the moon was high in the sky and it became obvious Evanna wasn't coming. He didn't despair. Acheson House must not have settled to sleep. The carriage could be hired again. Mrs Murray was hosting an entertainment that afternoon. He would find out the reason for Evanna's nonappearance when he saw her there and they could make new arrangements.

Only Evanna wasn't to be seen at Mrs Murray's, no more than was Lady Kerr, but it wasn't until another day had passed that Nathan could bear it no longer and called at Acheson House at the time the lady of the house would normally be 'at home'. When he presented his card he was shown into the study rather than the parlour. Lord Kerr was sat behind his desk studying a sheet of vellum. Nathan bowed. "I came to call on the ladies, sir. I mean no interruption to your business."

Lord Kerr did not rise to return his salutation but did lay the paper down on the desk and greet Nathan with a broad smile. "You will not find them here, I'm afraid. Evanna and her sisters are out with their mother buying frills and furbelows. You know how the ladies are when a bridal is in the air."

Unnerved by Lord Kerr's unaccustomed good humour, Nathan hesitated. "Ah…a wedding?"

The man's smile widened farther, and he waved an airy hand at the document on his desk. The script was clearly visible and easily read, Lord Kerr's gesture seemingly designed to draw Nathan's eye and facilitate his doing so. The written words stabbed his eyes. His brain did not want to accept them, but marriage contracts were not drawn up willy-nilly before negotiations were complete and agreed on. Nathan found he could find nothing to say except, "Ah… I see."

Lord Kerr rubbed his hands together and nodded towards a smaller note covered in spidery writing. "I was just composing the notice for the press. Lady Kerr and I will be issuing invitations to the nuptials shortly. We are delighted. Evanna will make a lovely bride. I expect she's selecting her gown at Madame Coeur's, her modiste, right now, as we speak."

Nathan's heart sank to his boots. Matters had obviously progressed past the point of no return. There was only one conclusion. Evanna might love him, but not enough to stand firm. He bowed stiffly. "Then you must pass on my good wishes for her future happiness. I bid you good day, sir."

He strode away from the house and averted his eyes from the front façade of the Temple as he walked past it. *My sweet love, I know they've pressured you into accepting this proposal, but could you not have held out just for me?*

Lord Kerr's words swirled around in his head. He couldn't bear it. It was an impossibility for him to be in Edinburgh and watch from the side lines as his true love married somebody else. An imagined family emergency would call for his instant return home to the Trossachs.

* * * *

Now

Nathan came out of his reverie with a soft smile.

By the time he'd reached his godfather's house his low spirits had been replaced with a foul mood at the unfairness of it all. He hadn't left Edinburgh with dignity so much as flounced off in a high dudgeon of youthful petulance. It was easy to see who his daughter, Cairstine, had inherited her flame-haired tempestuousness from. With the experience of years he would have handled the situation differently — except for making love to Evanna. That he would never regret nor wish to change.

He looked at the glass of brandy Cairstine had brought him and sipped. It had taken three years for his wounds to heal sufficiently to consider marriage to another. Cairstine's mother had been a gentle soul, and they'd been happy enough in the years they were together, until she was taken from them when Cairstine was seven. He'd had plenty of opportunities to marry again, especially when in the fullness of time he'd filled his father's shoes and his title had changed from Viscount McColl to the Duke of Glenard. He'd availed himself of none of them. He was content as he was. Life's lessons had taught him what he'd always known deep down — no woman could compare to Evanna.

He kept her silhouette at the back of a drawer in his desk. Over the years he'd tried not to gaze at it too often — the depth of his love for her still hurt should his unwary thoughts stray towards 'what if'. He'd never visited Edinburgh again either, knowing the pain he would feel should he come across Evanna in her married state. In fact, over the years he had heard not a word concerning her until tonight...

The door to his room crashed open, startling him. Duncan stepped over the threshold, his voice urgent. "Fire at the Armstrong house, Your Grace. We're organising a human chain to pass buckets of water from the well and extinguish the fire."

Nathan jumped to his feet and made haste to join the men in their work.

Chapter Eight

There was no lack of light to guide her footsteps as Evanna sped towards Armstrong House. Most of the town, oil lamps or torches in hand, were seemingly headed in the same direction. As she dodged between the rabble, their excited calls assailed her ears.

"It's well ablaze!"

"Reckon they'll 'av chucked the family silver outta the window to save it melting?"

"Easy pickin's if they has."

Is that all they can think about? Not that people's lives could be at risk? How callous. Although it was, she supposed, to be expected. Humdrum lives needed a little bit of excitement to relieve the grind of everyday hard work.

Evanna pushed her way through the crowd, the acrid smell of burning causing her eyes to water and her heart fill with terror. Then she saw him, highlighted in the flames of the conflagration, the pristine whiteness of his shirt covered with smuts of blackened ash, his face likewise sootily speckled. She shouted his name and ran to him, not caring that the rushing air flapped her pelisse open to reveal her nightgown to the notice of all and sundry. He looked up at the sound of her voice then opened his arms wide. Relief washed through her frame as she stepped into his embrace and sobbed onto his chest. "Nathan, I feared you were still inside."

He held her closer and kissed into the top of her hair. "There, there, my sweet. No harm done. I'm here."

My sweet? Still…?

Evanna's knees trembled, and she clung tighter. "I thought I had lost you again."

"Papa…?" Cairstine queried, a single word that held more than one question.

Nathan gently patted Evanna's back, soothing the last of her hiccupping sobs away as he turned to Cairstine. "You'll excuse me, child, if I leave you in your husband's care. I must escort Evanna home."

Cairstine's eyes widened as she stared at him before she smiled and kissed his cheek." I see you must. Take care, both of you."

Nathan nodded and kept his arm firmly around Evanna's waist as they walked away. Evanna lent on his support, enjoying the warmth of his nearness, scarce able to believe she and Nathan were walking together, side by side, once again. There was no mistaking the quiet happiness in his voice when he asked, "You could have knocked me over with a feather when I walked into Armstrong House and saw you there. How came you to be in Corbridge, my love? All these years I imagined you residing with your husband in Edinburgh. Is… Is…he here?"

My love!

Raven McAllan & Cassie O'Brien

Evanna's heart leapt, and although she wouldn't dream of talking so candidly of her widowhood to any other, this was Nathan. "No. He's dead, thank the Lord. He discovered in very short order I was not what he was looking for in a wife and exiled me to his property in Corbridge near as soon as we were wed. I've lived here ever since. Over twenty years now."

"He's dead?" Nathan sounded as inappropriately joyous to hear that news as Evanna herself felt about the fact. "I saw no notice of the fact in the press."

"No more did I. The first I heard of it was when his lawyer visited me in Corbridge ten years ago with papers from his heir ordering me to quit his property forthwith. A sudden fit of apoplexy carried him off apparently. My personal possessions, along with myself, were out on the street in less than two hours."

"Oh, Lord, Evanna! How did you manage? He left you a widow's portion, surely?"

"I suspected he would make my life a misery if he could so I acted and prepared accordingly." Evanna smiled wryly. "He left me nothing but his earnest hope that with his earthly legal obligations ended, I would end up the in the poorhouse, but as ever, he underestimated my resolve. He was so much older than me, and we parted on such bad terms, it was not a far stretch to guess this was coming my way. The marriage contract provided me with an annual amount of household expenses, along with a small personal allowance he could not escape paying. By careful management, I had enough put by to purchase the type of property that would also give me an income when he died, which incidentally, you will find two streets ahead, if you turn left now."

Walking against the stragglers still making their way to the scene of the fire, Nathan did so and asked, "Your parents did not step in to help you?"

Evanna tried to keep the bitterness from her voice but was not at all sure she succeeded. "I try not to be a person who bears grudge, it helps nothing and only leads to discontent, but after their treatment of me, I could never bring myself to speak to them again. They are as dead to me as the man they forced me to marry."

At her side, she felt Nathan stiffen. "Persuaded and manipulated, I guessed, but forced…?"

Evanna's jaw clenched at the memory, but she was determined to be honest and open. Nathan deserved that at least. "They imprisoned me in my room and fed me only a portion of bread and water each day until I agreed. I didn't like the man and they knew it. The pair of them sold me to get a daughter too many off their hands and to improve their own financial position."

Nathan stopped walking and turned her to face him. "I waited that night, and two days later, when I could no longer bear the not knowing, I called at Acheson House. Your father showed me the marriage contract and convinced me all concerned were delighted. That, as we spoke, you were out shopping for your bridal gown with your mother."

"I was upstairs behind a locked door, which as you know, was not facing the street, but at the back of the house. I waited by my window every night hoping you'd step into the garden so I could call down and explain."

Nathan's face creased in distress. "Your father was so sure of himself. I should have known!"

Evanna looked into his eyes and stroked her fingertips down the side of his face. "Do not place the weight of our years now on the shoulders of who we were then. You were but twenty and I eighteen. Young and in love we might have been, but we were no match for those pulling the strings behind the scenes."

Nathan bent his head as if he were going to kiss her, but if that was his intention, it was foiled by the appearance of Sydney, who skidded around the corner with his fast-guttering torch. "It weren't me, Mrs P. Honest it weren't. By the time I got there the flames was already lickin' outta the windows. 'onest!"

She chucked him under his chin. "Of course it wasn't. Run ahead and light our way with what you've got, Sydney. Maisie'll find you a bed with the kitchen lads."

Sydney's lip trembled, but he did was he was bid. Nathan looked at her enquiringly as they followed on. "Mrs P? Cairstine called you that too?"

She shrugged. "The full-length alternative is one I detest. I've made a life for myself in Corbridge as a solitary woman. I encourage the abbreviation. Few people remember my full name these days. Thankfully."

Nathan squeezed his arm around her waist. "What did he do to you, sweetheart? Was it that bad?"

"I try not to think about it, but…let's say it was to be endured." Evanna's mind, as ever, shied away from the memory, but she admitted what she could. "After what we overheard in the Temple, I thought the physical aspect of marriage to him wouldn't actually take place. But it did. And his demands were…unpleasant, to say the least."

She was saved from adding any further detail as her home hove into view. Most of her staff were milling around outside of the open front door. Maisie spotted them first. "There you are, Madam P. What on earth is going on? We didn't even know you had returned from Denny House until you dashed down the stairs and out of the front door like a mad thing. It gave us quite a fright."

That she was receiving a scolding from her maid bothered Evanna not one bit. Maisie had done more for her than any other person ever had. She might be an employee but she was also a friend, and the proprieties normally observed between servant and mistress did not exist.

"I had to go and see what was occurring. The young lady I was chaperoning was at Armstrong House earlier this evening, as was her father. They might have needed help. Luckily my help was not needed, and Cairstine's father has kindly escorted me home after I found them both safe and sound."

Maisie crossed herself. "Thank the Lord, none have perished."

Evanna felt Nathan's arm tighten around her waist and glanced up at him. "Except the baron," he said. "I'm afraid he ran back inside and so fierce was the inferno none could follow to save him."

There were several gasps from the assembled staff.

"He had not recovered the use of his wits?" Evanna ventured in a quiet undertone they would not be able to hear and speculate upon.

"Unfortunately not," Nathan confirmed, equally softly. "The man was naked as a jay and waving a brandy bottle when he disappeared into the flames."

"His poor son. He witnessed it, I presume?"

"He did. Duncan and Cairstine will take George back with them to Denny House and provide what comfort they can."

Evanna clasped Nathan's hand. "Come along in. You must be in need of a restorative yourself."

He smiled. "Aye, love. I must admit a large dram and a wee cuddle wouldn't go amiss."

To Nathan's delight, Evanna's entrancing dimple appeared at his words. It had been so long since he'd seen it! The intervening years had wrought a few changes on them both. His hair was white at the temples, his waistline was not so slim. Her hair contained silver threads, the fine lines around her eyes were deeper, but any weight she'd gained had settled just where it should be so far as he was concerned.

Her staff goggled as she took his hand, and none more so than the outspoken maid, who, if he was not mistaken, was as Scottish as he and Evanna were themselves. She murmured as Evanna led him in. "Ach, I'll run ahead. If you excuse yourself from the parlour, I'll have a day dress ready to replace your bedgown."

Evanna paused and smiled into the woman's worried eyes. "Do you remember at Acheson House, Maisie? All those years ago, when you delivered a note for me to a certain Viscount McColl?"

The maid's face creased into a moue of disgust. "He wasn't there. Then you had to marry that Sassenach swine... Although now I come to think on it, those times being not being such as I care to recall, that's the same clan name as the young lass as you've been chaperoning?"

Evanna squeezed his hand. "Viscount McColl is now the Duke of Glenard, and yes Maisie, he is also Lady Cairstine's father."

Maisie's mouth dropped open and she scowled. Evidently his upgrade in title made little impression on her. She folded her arms across her chest and eyed him beadily. "So you finally turned up, did you? Took you a while."

Evanna answered softly, "Another circumstance engineered by my parents, it seems."

This short sentence apparently explained every-thing. Maisie's face cleared. "Aye. I'll go shoo the staff back to bed, then."

"Could you find one for Sydney?"

The woman nodded and disappeared back through the front door, the informality of the exchange between her and Evanna telling Nathan that although plainly garbed as befitted a servant, he might have mistaken Maisie's position. She obviously stood higher in Evanna's affections than a mere member of her household staff.

Evanna's house, like most in Corbridge, was built of honey-coloured stone blocks stood four-square on the street, and he breathed in the scent of lavender and beeswax as he stepped over the threshold. The silence of the hall was broken only by the sonorous tick that could be heard from the grandfather clock in the corner of the hall and a few shouts from the scene of the fire a few streets away.

Oil lamps lit the interior. The rise of the stairs was to his left with several closed doors ranged around them. Evanna stepped onto the first tread. "The house is a little quiet with my girls away. Come up, my private apartment is on the first floor."

Evanna's use of the possessive seemed to suggest her marriage had lasted long enough for her to have borne children, so Nathan posed the question. "*Your* girls?"

Evanna smiled. "My income is derived from the young lady boarders who attend the local seminary. They have returned to their parents for the summer and will come back to me when term resumes in September. The house is very different then. Busy, lively with their chatter, and I adore it."

That no child had been conceived was for the best, so far as Nathan was concerned. Maternal instinct aside, the unfortunate infant would have been a life-long reminder of the man Evanna hated. "I'm glad they provide you with such good company, then."

Evanna opened the door to a lamplit room. Her bed and armoire were screened to one side of it and in front of a large bay window was a sitting room arrangement of a comfortable sofa and low table. She waved an airy hand towards the fireplace as she led him in. "My girls are with me for three years before they return home to begin an adult life of their own. We become close and stay in contact. I may have borne no babes, but still my mantlepiece is full of invitations to engagements, weddings and christenings. Already I have half a dozen godchildren. Sit and I will fetch us both a dram."

He did so and accepted the crystal tumbler of amber liquid she offered him. "I am widowed myself as well. Emily died of puerile fever when Cairstine was seven years old."

She sat beside him and sipped. "So I gathered from your daughter, and I will admit it was the name that tempted me to accept an appointment to chaperone the Lady Cairstine McColl for a few weeks over the summer."

Nathan smiled. "I didn't marry for three years after we parted, until my father stepped up the pressure for me to provide an heir. Cairstine will inherit my lands and worldly goods, and although the Glenard title will become extinct, I had no inclination to sire more children, nor marry again to anyone who was not you."

Evanna snuggled into his side. "Nor I."

He set his glass down and slipped his arm around her shoulders. She looked into his eyes and lifted her face to his. Her lips were as soft as he remembered, and her kiss as sweet. Her nipples pressed against the fine cotton of her nightgown, and he brushed his fingertips over them. Her breath whispered as their lips parted, "Be gentle with me please…"

Just what did that brute do to her?

He continued to lightly stroke, his cock hardening inside his breeches. "Take charge, then? Ride me?"

She cupped his throbbing balls. "How?"

Evanna being as eager as he, Nathan pulled off his shirt, shrugged off his breeches and released his cock. "Straddle me. Take my shaft inside you according to your own desire."

She sighed and did so, her wet channel sinking down inch by inch on his hard length. He grasped her buttocks as she began to rock, the globes of her breasts more beautifully generous than ever, undulating against his chest as she moved. Evanna bounced harder, and he moaned with the longing to cup her breast and take her nipple into his mouth. She had liked it on the only other time they'd made love. But now?

He need not have worried. She lifted her breast to his mouth. Overjoyed, he circled her nipple with his tongue, gently licking, kissing, until she mewled. "Yes, more…"

He sucked then, keeping his teeth well away, his balls threatening to explode. Her fingertips dug into his shoulder as she ground down and cried out. "Yes... Nathan..."

He could hold on no longer and groaned out his own ecstasy. "Evanna...my, sweet love..."

Nathan held her close while their ragged breathing steadied. Full night had fallen, and the glass of the window appeared black except in the centre, where like looking into a mirror, the glow of the lamp light reflected their entwined figures. He sighed, enjoying the sight of them naked—Evanna facing him, straddling his lap, her head resting on his shoulder, her hair loosened, tumbling down her back.

Her back?

He ran his fingers through the silky strands, parting them, and swallowed hard at what the reflection showed him. Thin white lines criss-crossed her skin in a pattern that gave tell as to what must have inflicted them. He held her tighter and traced his fingertip down the length of one. "Evanna, sweetheart, how did you come by these?"

She buried her face in his neck. "My wedding night is not one I care to recall. To do so revolts me. No one but Maisie knows I bear these marks, and it is by her hand that my scars are not deeper."

Nathan's throat tightened. "He did this to you? Percival-Smyth?"

She did not answer but with a small sob burrowed deeper.

With effort, Nathan managed to prevent his fingers from curling into fists. "Will you tell me?"

She lifted her head and wiped away the tear trickling down her cheek. "For you, and only you, I will. Just once... Then the subject must never be raised again. What happened cannot be changed, and I made the choice long ago not to allow memories of that night to infect my life by dwelling on them."

Nathan kissed the tip of her nose. "Perhaps another dram might be in order?"

Evanna reached for her nightgown and eased herself from his lap. "I believe you may be right."

Reclothed, they sat once more side by side on the sofa. He rested his arm around her shoulders and waited. She sipped and stared into the far distance. "To stop and start would be difficult. It will go easier for me if I may relay events straight through without interruption?"

"I promise to bite my tongue until you give me leave."

Evanna's hand shook as she raised her glass, but she sipped resolutely then began.

"The morning after we'd visited the Temple my parents informed me of Percival-Smyth's proposal. I told them I had no intention of marrying the man no matter how much money was on offer. Isolated and starved into submission from that moment up until the day I married, that time is blurry, like sleepwalking through a bad dream from which I woke to the living nightmare that was my wedding night…"

She swallowed hard. "Percival-Smyth made it clear, as his wife, he considered my body was his to command. He jabbed and poked and pinched and bit, then crowed like a cock on a dung heap after he reached his satisfaction — until he saw no sign of his taking my maidenhead. He ordered me to kneel at his feet and beg his forgiveness, but I told him I would *never* apologise for the love we had shared, and in return, I took him to task for his treatment of me…"

The words shot out of Nathan's mouth before he couldn't stop them. "The bastard!"

Evanna shuddered. "If I thought Percival-Smyth was angry before, it was like nothing to the fury my response invoked. As judge and jury he declared me guilty. I was a woman of abhorrent morals and my punishment for such was written in law…"

Oh, God! No! 'To be publicly whipped at the cart's tail until thy back be bloody'.

"He secured my hands to the bedpost. I was to consider myself fortunate. My corporal correction would be administered by himself in private. At the end, when his riding switch had done its worse, he strode from the room. How long he would have left me there, bound and bleeding, I don't know…"

Bile rose in Nathan's throat. "It is as well the bastard is already dead!"

Evanna squeezed his hand. "But Percival-Smyth didn't know that I'm caurie-fisted. My left hand is dexterous. The cord binding it was slightly looser. I managed to pick at the knots at my wrist, free myself and ring for Maisie. She came running to me, and so far as I'm concerned her actions saved my life. She tended my wounds and kept them clean, ensuring they remained free of infection, and brought food to my room. She guarded my door with fierceness of a hunting dog and allowed no one in. When I emerged some weeks later it was to a cold interview. Mr Percival-Smyth never wanted to set eyes on such a disgusting creature as me in the foreseeable future, or indeed, ever. I was dispatched to Corbridge. He never spoke to me again, nor I him, and that's the way it remained until the day he died."

"My sweet love, I never knew…"

Evanna shushed him with a kiss on his lips. "Of course you didn't. How could you?"

A little comforted, Nathan kissed her back. "But your life afterward was not so bad?"

"No man has been near me, by my choice. Having experienced hell with him and heaven with you, I wanted nothing unless…you know." Her dimple peeped out as she wiggled on his lap. "I can assure you I am now a very respectable widow, although at the moment, possibly not so much…"

He chuckled. "Not for much longer, I hope. There are no obstacles in our path. We can be married as soon as we wish." He looked uncertain. "If you wish?"

She gazed into his eyes. "I wish for it very much, but you will have to forgive me, not so soon. Corbridge and my young ladies gave me back my life. I can abandon neither until my contractual obligation ceases at the end of this academic year."

"Then I will take over the lease of Denny House and provide what assistance I can to George whilst we set the town's ears alight with news of our courtship."

"And I will train my successor to take up the reins."

"Maisie?" he guessed.

Evanna smiled. "There will be nobody better."

Nathan agreed, and a thought occurred. "If we are to conduct a formally long-winded path to the altar, I would like the ceremony to be conducted with due pomp in Edinburgh with enough noise to garner a column or several in the Scottish national press. By that method the news should make its way to the ears of a certain elderly couple in Kerr Castle that they were wrong to keep us apart. Very wrong indeed."

Evanna wrapped her arms around his neck, her beautiful breasts squashed against his chest. "Yes, my love. I would like that very much too."

Chapter Nine

Eighteen months later…

Evanna waved goodbye to the last of 'her girls' and gave a happy sigh.

The end of an era and the start of a new one.

With Nathan.

Once the heavily laden carriage had turned the corner, she closed the door of her house and leant on it.

No more cheerful chatter of young ladies, eager — or not — to discover the intricacies of the ton, men and adulthood. No more tears and tantrums, no more fads and fancies to worry about. Everything would be down to Maisie now.

She would miss it all, Evanna admitted, but not nearly so much as she could have done, because she was finally marrying the love of her life.

"Mrs P, are you quite well?" The anxious voice of Sydney — since the fire he'd become firmly affixed to her household — brought her out of her reverie.

Evanna pulled herself together and smiled at him. "Yes, Sydney. You caught me wool-gathering for a moment or two. Now, is your box packed? Including the new livery you will wear to work for His Grace?"

"It's gonna be strange, you being a countess. Havin' to learn to call you sommat else like."

He scowled and Evanna was hard-pressed not to laugh at his expression.

"What if I gets it wrong an' calls you Mrs P instead?"

Evanna ruffled his hair. "It's not a hanging offence. I dare say when people address me as the countess or my lady, I'll be looking about to see who they are talking to."

"Be different, but good different, I fink. A castle an' countryside, an' I get to work wiv' the 'orses in Scotland..." He looked suddenly stricken. "I won't have to wear one of them there kilts will I, Mrs P? Bet they're awful draughty."

Evanna schooled herself not to laugh. Poor Sydney, it was obvious the thought bothered him. She hastened to reassure him. "Of course not. Your new livery has breeches, doesn't it? At other times you will wear the clothes you've brought with you and are used to. Given time, you never know, you might even fancy wearing one. In the appropriate tartan of course."

He looked horrified. "Me? Show me knees? What if there's a breeze? They'll all see me bits and pieces.? No, ta. I'll keep me keck on."

Evanna couldn't help it. She laughed. "Oh, Sydney, a kilt is designed *not* to show your, ah, nether regions. That's why it's made of nine whole yards of material. It's heavy. It doesn't blow around in the wind." Because if it did there would be a lot of swooning, scandalised or aroused ladies all over the place. She chose not to share that titbit. "However, I promise you will never be forced to wear highland dress of any kind."

Evanna ruffled his hair again and sent him on his way. "Off with you, then. I'm sure you have work to do, as have I."

She headed for her day office to find Maisie sitting behind what up until that point had been Evanna's desk. Maisie started to rise and Evanna waved her down. "No. It is your place now."

Maisie gave her a rueful smile. "I'm not sure there's a woman alive that can fill your shoes, let alone me."

"Pish." Evanna dismissed Maisie's doubts with an airy wave of her hand. "You've been one step behind me for the nigh on twenty years, since I took in my first boarder. You are more than capable of running this house and the seminary are happy to recommend pupils continue board here under your care and guidance."

"To think I couldn't even read and write when we first came here."

Maisie had expressed an interest in learning her letters not long after their arrival in Corbridge, and Evanna had been delighted to oblige. She had proved an apt pupil. A copy of a Shakespeare play currently stood on the night table beside her bed and her neat figurework was displayed on the pages of the ledger laid on the desk.

"And now you can do both as well as me. Do not do yourself down, Maisie. You are an educated woman equipped with the means and skills necessary to make your own way through life according to your own design. Stand proud. You've worked hard and you deserve it."

"Because of you."

It was not something they had talked about often, or even at all in recent years, both preferring to put the events of her marriage to Mr Percival-Smyth behind them — but with this being the last time she and Maisie would be in each other's company for the foreseeable future, Evanna wanted to acknowledge her debt. "Because of both of us. You wouldn't be in this position if you hadn't met me, I wouldn't be here without the care you gave me when I was so grievously injured."

Maisie jumped to her feet to give Evanna a hug and there was a hint of nostalgic sadness in the smile they exchanged, but both of them knew it was time to move on. Time to say goodbye.

Evanna rang the bell and instructed Sydney to run to Denny House with a message for His Grace. Maisie squared her shoulders and followed her into the hall to wave her off.

* * * *

Nathan tried to curb his impatience as he peered out onto the street through the drawing room window of Denny House. His rental of the property had been duly terminated, and once the longed-for message arrived he would finally be able shake the dust of Corbridge off his feet for good. Not that he bore any grudge to either the house or the town, how could he when they had reunited him with his true love, but it was time to return to Scotland with Evanna at his side and begin their life together, married and living under the same roof.

Sydney ran around the corner, puffing hard. Nathan walked into the hall, where a line of staff waited to make their farewells. A breathless Sydney appeared at the front door. "Mrs P says as she's ready, Your Grace."

Nathan's coach and four awaited on the street with his trunk strapped to its roof. The household bowed or curtsied as he walked past them, and he was handed his hat and cane by the major-domo at the door. In return he gave the man a white pound note he took from his pocket. "If you would be so good as to purchase a barrel of beer and one of porter for the kitchen so the staff may toast my forthcoming marriage?"

"It will be an honour, Your Grace, to raise a cheer. On behalf of the household, may I say, it has been our privilege to serve you, and we offer our very best wishes for your future happiness."

Nathan inclined his head to accept the sentiment then with a light tread stepped out of the door with Sydney at his heels. "You may ride on the box with the coachman, laddie."

Sydney grinned and hopped up. The footman opened the door for Nathan to climb aboard then jumped onto the backboard as the coachman cracked his whip. Nathan's spirits were ebullient as the horses responded. It had been, in parts, a wonderful year. To come across Evanna so unexpectedly and find she still loved him, and he, her. Then, six months ago, his darling daughter Cairstine and her husband Duncan had presented him with his first grandchild. A wee boy, James Alastair, also known by one of Duncan's lesser titles, the Marquess of Ettrick. As a finale he had recently received a letter from his good friend, George Armstrong, Baron Renfew, announcing his marriage to a beautiful widow, Mrs Grace Foston.

In other ways though, his time at Denny House had been somewhat of a trial. Due to Evanna's long-standing commitments, they had lived separately, giving an outward show of respectable courtship with any intimate moments having to be snatched, when and if, the opportunity arose. It would be nothing but a relief to be rid of such subterfuge and be able to conduct their relationship openly, in full view of the public gaze.

The coachman pulled up outside Evanna's residence. Nathan did not descend, forgoing the social niceties in order for the two of them to get underway without delay. His footmen hefted her trunk onto the roof as Evanna entered the coach and made herself comfortable on the squabs of the seat. Outside on the street Maisie dabbed her eyes on her handkerchief then used it to wave farewell when the vehicle rocked into motion once more.

Evanna blew her nose into her own square of linen. "It feels odd be leaving Maisie here, but she deserves her chance."

Nathan squeezed her hand. "That she does, my love. She has been a sterling support to you, I know, but I'm here now and you may trust me to do so in her place."

Evanna smiled a little tremulously, then resolutely screwed her sodden hankie into a tight ball and stuffed it in her pocket. "I know it. I'm just being daft…"

Nathan twitched the curtains shut at the window and opened his arms. "Come here. Snuggle in."

She wriggled closer and Nathan held her to his chest.

"This is the most comfortable carriage I've ever ridden in." She sighed.

Her soft breasts pressed against him, and as ever, Nathan's shaft hardened. "I'm not sure comfortable is exactly how I would describe myself right now."

She glanced at his lap and giggled. "Nathan..."

Her fingers traced the outline of his cock over the material of his breeches. He kissed her firmly, slid his hand under the neckline of her gown and stroked the top of her breast. Their tongues entwined, her hand fondled his crotch until he gasped. "You will unman me shortly, my love."

She chuckled, her voice low and throaty. "The side curtains are closed and we have at least two hours before we change horses. The road is uneven and if I sit on your lap, we could have a pleasurable ride in more ways than one."

Nathan groaned with longing. To his joy Evanna's past no longer haunted her, and she had become more confident in their lovemaking over the past year. She took him wherever and whenever she could, and he loved her for it. "Yes, please, my love."

She lifted the hem of her travelling gown just enough to give him a quick glimpse of her silk stocking-clad legs. He wondered just how high her garters were and his fingers sought the top of the lacy garments. With one swift movement, she turned and lifted herself to sit on his lap facing him. His cock threatened to burst through his breeches. She gazed into his eyes and bit her lip before she freed his cock and raised her hips.

"Yes, now, love... Please."

She grasped his staff and guided him into her warm wetness, sinking down until he was penetrating her deep inside her channel. The sensation was exquisite and he groaned. She began to move. Synchronised with the bumping carriage, the sensation was amazing.

Evanna rocked and ground, her face alight with the sheer joy of their union, then she began to move faster. Nathan used one hand to hold her upright and slid the other under her skirts to caress her sensitive nub. She moaned, a series of small mewls of pleasure, her fingers tightening and digging into his shoulders signalling the arrival of her climax. He shuddered, his seed erupting from his cock-head and filling her with warmth. "Perfect, my love. So perfect…"

Breathing hard, Evanna laid her head on his shoulder and he kissed into her hair. They clung together, enjoying the afterglow of their lovemaking until the coach wheels bumped over a large rut and the sway of the carriage made Nathan aware it must have turned off the main highway.

He reached into his pocket and handed Evanna his handkerchief. "As much as I would like to clean you, slowly, lovingly, I believe we are about to stop to change the horses. A private parlour has been reserved for us at each of the four stages we require to complete our journey to Edinburgh. If you're in need of the facilities before we head on?"

Evanna slid off him and began to tidy herself. "Thank you. I will."

Nathan nudged the window curtain an inch to one side and peered out to confirm his summation of the journey so far. An ostler ran from the inn — the golden gilt of his ducal crest decorating the doors of the vehicle having attracted immediate attention. "A-hey…a-hey…coachman to me."

Their carriage halted as Evanna shook her skirts to cover her legs. Nathan fully opened the curtain, signalling the footman he had permission to open the door. A popular staging post on the highway to

Edinburgh, several other coaches were pulled up, their occupants milling around the yard. The inn lad bustled forward cutting a swathe through the crowd. "Make way, make way, make way for His Grace."

The hum of chatter increased as people turned to stare, but one querulous voice caught Nathan's attention as he poked his head outside.

"Robina, attend me at once. You know full well I cannot descend without my stick. Why is it not to hand?"

Sharper and certainly more elderly than he remembered, still there was no mistaking to whom the voice belonged, and he heard Evanna's sharp intake of breath behind him. He looked back over his shoulder, and she shook her head, no. He faced front again and clicked his fingers at the lad. "We will remain here during this stop. Bring two drams of your finest while the horses are being exchanged."

"Yes, yer Grace. Course, yer Grace." The lad bowed and ran off to do as he'd been bid.

Evanna leant back into the corner of the coach when she recognised her mother's voice. That her parent happened to be in the same inn at the same time as herself might just have been an unlucky coincidence, but it was certainly an unwelcome surprise. She took a deep breath in, grateful not to have been taken unawares and walked bang into her mother.

Nathan handed her a pottery tumbler when the tray was presented to him, then pulled the door shut and closed the curtain, restoring their privacy once more. "Well, that was unexpected. And on the road that leads to Edinburgh, too. Could it be that notice of our forthcoming marriage printed in the *Scottish Times* last week has already stirred the pot? Mayhap she's seeking a reconciliation?"

The fiery spirit of the amber liquid warmed Evanna's throat as she swallowed. "I can't imagine what plausible reason she could offer for suddenly wishing to re-enter my life after an absence of more than twenty years. I wilfully cut my connection with them, but not once in the intervening time did they reach out to me either."

"But if she sent your sister to you in her place?"

Evanna considered the matter. "For fairness' sake I would hear Robina out, but if she came solely as my mother's emissary my stance would remain the same. However, if she appealed to me on her own behalf because her life is in no way happy, I would offer her my aid to escape their influence, should she wish it."

"By…?"

She smiled as the obvious solution occurred, then presented him with her *fait accompli*. "By sending her to Maisie, of course. I would not put it past my parents to make a very public fuss in an attempt to force a monetary settlement if we offer her shelter, but a respectable house for young lady boarders in an out-of-the-way town would not attract the same attention. Robina is several years over her majority, so they could do nothing about it, and you can be sure Maisie would not allow either of my parents over the doorstep should they arrive in person and attempt to coerce her to return home."

Nathan chuckled and tipped the remaining contents of his tumbler down his throat. "Then our plan is made. If either of your parents dares to approach they will receive the cut direct, but Robina, if unaccompanied, will be invited to speak her piece."

Evanna finished her whisky and Nathan threw the tumblers back out of the door with a silver shilling for the boy.

* * * *

At the next change Nathan handed her out of the coach and they used the facilities but did not linger. By the following stop, they estimated they had made enough ground on the Kerr coach to enable a longer pause to eat.

The landlord welcomed them with a smile and his assurance of their private parlour being ready to receive them. "A nice mutton stew, roast chicken and a hearty apple pie will be with you in a trice. With some ale or perhaps a glass of the wife's dandelion wine to go with it?"

"Perfect," Evanna said gratefully. It had been quite some while since breakfast.

Nathan seemed as hungry as she. He rubbed his hands together. "Lead us to it."

Evanna admitted she would be glad to arrive at their destination as she tucked in. "I anticipated Corbridge to Edinburgh in one sprint would be quite an undertaking, but even in a carriage as luxurious as yours, eleven hours on the road once the changes are included is proving to be a harder slog than I'd realised."

Nathan carved her a leg of chicken and placed it on her plate. "It'll be worth it when we're tucked up snug as a bug in a rug at Acheson House tonight."

Evanna smiled impishly. Wherever the Kerr's Edinburgh destination might be it was not in the residence they had previously rented. His Grace The

Duke of Glenard had reserved that right for himself. "Will the Temple still be there, do you think? We should pay it a visit, if so."

He smirked and so did she—both of them twenty years younger at that moment. "We most certainly will. For the rest, you will have your room, I mine, and what we do between ourselves is nobody's business but ours so far as I'm concerned. The banns have been called. We marry on Saturday. Cairstine and Duncan arrive tomorrow, George and Grace the day after. In such a busy household there will be little scope for tattling servants to note our comings and goings."

Cairstine and Duncan, Evanna knew well, likewise George, but his marriage to Grace was so recent neither she nor Nathan had yet met his bride, and she looked forward to doing so. Two children would accompany the couples. Nathan's baby grandson, James, and George's newly adopted daughter, Georgina. With them as well as their nursemaids, Acheson House was about to become a very lively place indeed.

* * * *

And so it proved. Travel worn and weary, Evanna spent her first whole night snuggled against the warm body of the man she loved. They had picked his room to sleep in for the discretion of his long-serving valet, Dougie, who could be trusted to not bat so much as an eyelid, nor to breath a word when he opened the curtains and let daylight into the room to find his master in bed with his 'not yet wed' betrothed.

He set Nathan's jug of hot shaving water down on the washstand then bowed. "May I fetch your morning drink, ma'am? A tea, perhaps? Or a hot chocolate?"

Evanna stretched and reached for her wrap. "No, but you could poke your head out of the door and keep watch down the hallway while I run back to my room in case my chambermaid puts in appearance before I do?"

Dougie's eyes twinkled as he did what he was bid. Evanna slipped out of bed and fastened her wrap over her nightgown then whisked herself back to her unslept-in bed. She slipped beneath the covers not three minutes before the door opened to admit a maid she didn't recognise — not unsurprisingly, as after twenty years, not one member of the original staff of Acheson House remained, although the property itself was largely unchanged.

For her own personal use, Evanna had chosen the bedroom of her first visit. She had experienced the happiest of times there as well as the worst. The reasoning behind her and Nathan choosing to stay at Acheson House being to reinforce the remembrance of their first tender feelings for each other and to overlay any bad memories with those of the final consummation of their love. So far it was working. She was excited to discover if the tinkling music still played at night, but it didn't matter if not. She and Nathan would laugh about it anyway.

The chambermaid carried a steaming cup of hot chocolate and bobbed her curtsey after she set it down on the nightstand beside the bed. "I'm Janet, ma'am. Here to answer your bell should you require my assistance during your stay."

Evanna smiled her thanks. She thought she ought to set about appointing a lady's maid — the ceremonial duties of a duchess being somewhat more onerous than those of even the most respectable Mrs Anybody-From-

Anywhere. It would be strictly a professional appointment though — there was only one Maisie, after all.

In preparation for her new role she had commissioned several gowns on rather fancier lines than she'd been accustomed to wear of late. None were up to the standard of Madame Coeur's creations, but the fabric was of the finest quality, and the needlework of the local Corbridge seamstress very neatly done. Evanna indicated her trunk, as yet unpacked as they had arrived so late. "If you would locate and lay out fresh undergarments and my green sprigged muslin, you may deal with the rest later this morning."

Janet bobbed again then bustled about her task. Evanna drank her chocolate and contemplated the day to come. She was looking forward to seeing Cairstine again.

* * * *

Nathan watched Evanna whisk herself out of the door then requested Dougie to lay out his daywear and retrieve him the latest edition of the *Scottish Times* from the hall table while he dressed. He returned with it in time to assist Nathan in the tying of his cravat and Nathan sat on the bedroom chair to peruse the newspaper after his valet left the room.

The society pages were what he sought, and as he'd hoped, his eye soon alighted on a paragraph in which a recent ball held at the Assembly Room was notated. A certain Mrs Mhairi McPherson was still a patroness, it seemed. *Good.* Young Sydney would shortly be dispatched to the Assembly Rooms in search of her address. Once in possession of this information,

Sydney would then pay a visit to the back door of the residence named and enquire whether Lady Kerr had arrived, for it seemed likely to Nathan that as the Kerr coach had only contained his future mother-in-law and Robina, they would not be renting a house, but staying with a person with whom they had a close acquaintance.

A negative answer might still illicit the correct address for her but if, as Nathan suspected, Lady Kerr was there, she would receive a visit from himself, and if she mistook him for the same easily palmed-off man he had been twenty years ago, then more fool her. With icy politeness, he intended to leave her in no doubt of the inadvisability of contacting the eldest daughter she had treated so shamefully, and with prospect to warm him, he re-folded the paper and walked downstairs with a bounce in his step. His grandson would be arriving in the company of his parents in just a few hours, and Nathan was looking forward to seeing how much the babe had grown in the three months since he'd last seen him.

Evanna was already sitting at the table when he entered the dining room, and in front of the hovering servants he greeted her as if they hadn't just spent the night in each other's arms. "Good morning, my dearest. Did you sleep well?"

Playing the game as well as he, Evanna's dimple appeared. "Very well, I thank you. Have you any plans for us today?"

With his wish for the occasion to cause a stir, over one hundred guests had been invited to bear witness to their marriage ceremony at Edinburgh's High Kirk Cathedral, with a wedding banquet being held at the Assembly Rooms after. However, with the bride and groom being widow and widower, they had decided the service itself should be simple affair without bridal attendants or groomsmen or choir. Evanna would walk down the aisle on Nathan's arm and the minister would conduct the shortened version of the service in its simplest form.

"Cairstine, Duncan and wee James were to spend the night at their last change in Linlithgow so should be with us around midday. As the arrangements thus far have been made in writing, I thought in the meantime to pay a call at St. Giles' and discuss the final detail of the order of service for Saturday?"

Evanna set her knife and fork down on her plate and dabbed her lips on her napkin. "I hope the minister will not mind our not having the full triumphal entry of the bride accompanied by organ and choir."

Nathan drank the last of his coffee. "I daresay we're not the first widow and widower he's married in a quieter manner without fanfare."

Sydney, in his new role of pageboy, entered the dining room and presented Evanna with her bonnet. "Let alone those 'e's 'ad to wed in a rush cos the bride's up the duff, Mrs P."

Two audible intakes of breath were heard from the resident major-domo and maid. Evanna blushed a little — presumably for Sydney's parochial manners. Nathan hid his smile and, much amused, only reproved him mildly. "Insightful, Sydney, but perhaps a thought best kept to yourself."

"Righty-o, yer Graceness," Sydney chirped, not one wit perturbed.

Evanna tied the ribbons of her bonnet, and Nathan escorted her out into the fresher air of the street, noting that as well as being discomforted by Sydney's cheeky remark, the dining room must have been over-warm, for her face was still quite pink.

Nathan handed Evanna into the coach, and she settled back onto the squabs still feeling warmth on her cheeks.

Out of the mouths of babes…

Had Sydney just hit the nail on the head? She rather suspected he might have. It had taken quite some while for the possibility to push its way into her mind, the consequences of enjoying intimacy with a man being something she hadn't had to consider for years on end until she and Nathan had renewed their love. Evanna led a busy life and the absence of her monthly courses had slipped by largely unnoticed, until the recent departure of her young lady boarders had allowed her some leisure for contemplation a few days ago.

Four months…and nearing five…

No nausea had so far afflicted her, and that her breasts were tender she had put down to the enthusiasm of Nathan's lovemaking, but then, over the last week or so there had also been a fluttering, bubbling sensation in her belly.

A baby…?

It didn't seem possible. She had long suppressed all maternal longings to bear a child of her own. As a widow in possession of a fine townhouse and an income, she'd attracted the attention of a gentleman or two who'd indicated they would like to know her better, but after the treatment she had suffered at her late husband's hands it had not been a prospect she could contemplate.

Until Nathan…

What would people say if her belly started to noticeably swell? The marriage of a respectable widow would be presumed for companionship, not the bedroom games that led to said widow conceiving a child at the grand old age of thirty-eight. There would be knowing looks and titters, she suspected.

Nathan climbed into the coach and made himself comfortable beside her. This child, if indeed it proved a reality, would be younger than his grandson. Would it perturb him? She glanced sideways at the profile of the man she loved.

No, she was sure it wouldn't, and steadied by this thought her practical nature came to the fore. She had no clue how one went about getting a pregnancy confirmed, or not, but other women did. A discreet question or two would show her the way and until then there was no point in fretting Nathan with a prospect that might still be the product of an overexcited imagination.

Her composure regained, she was able to ask in a perfectly normal manner, "The harpist you engaged to play softly in the background has confirmed her attendance though?"

"She has." Nathan smiled. "I suggest a little Mozart along with Handel's harp solo from *Passacagalia* would be suitable for the occasion?"

Music not being Evanna's forte, she was happy to go along with Nathan's choice. "Lovely. Then this afternoon, once the babe and his staff have settled into the nursery, you could call at the Assembly Rooms with Duncan whilst I visit the milliner's with Cairstine to select my wedding bonnet?"

Nathan winked. "An onerous duty, my love, but someone has to do it. The wines to be served at our wedding celebration need to be sampled for taste and quality beforehand."

Evanna nudged his arm. "Do not become too merry, my lord. I have plans for us later tonight."

Nathan chuckled and the coach pulled up outside the kirk. A solitary verger was sweeping the aisle when they entered, so Nathan presented his card and requested it be taken to the reverend. In short order, they were escorted to the vestry where the minister proved accommodating to all their requests, especially when Nathan handed over the coins the organist and choir would have been due to receive had they been called on to perform their normal duties.

Luncheon was served on their return to Acheson House, and it was not long after they'd finished eating when a keffufle in the hall heralded the arrival of the Earl and Countess of Callander. Nathan jumped to his feet as Cairstine carried wee James in through the door. He kissed his daughter and grandson soundly then clasped his hand in Duncan's.

Cairstine walked closer and offered out James with a smile. "Would you care to hold him, Mrs P?"

The mechanics of actually producing a child being outside her experience, Evanna's godmotherly duties nevertheless allowed her to take the babe into her arms with confidence and coo, "There now, wee man. You're here safe and sound. Shall we go and find your nursery? Your mama would like to see it, I'm sure."

The babe gurgled and Cairstine smiled. "Yes, let's get him settled. He's been restive this last leg of the journey and I'm sure could do with an hour in his crib."

Evanna stood with James in her arms. Nathan walked to the sideboard and looked at Duncan. "A restorative to recover from the journey?"

"I'll admit a wee dram would not go amiss."

Cairstine huffed and raised her eyes heavenward. "Men! Straight for the decanter."

Duncan grinned. "Don't tell me you won't be grateful to find a wee glass of amber gold sat beside your chair when you get back from settling our son."

"Make sure there is then," Cairstine shot over her shoulder as she followed Evanna from the room.

James' nursemaid accompanied them up the stairs, and Evanna opened the door to what had been on her previous stay at Acheson House Catriona and Marietta's bedroom. Light and airy with double aspect windows, it was situated on the far side of the house, quiet and peaceful in its isolation from the main reception rooms on the floor below.

Evanna kissed the babe's downy head and handed him to the nursemaid. His mother stroked his cheek then threaded her arm through Evanna's as they made their way back to the men. "Dear Mrs P. I'm in a quandary. What shall I call you after the wedding when you won't be Mrs P anymore? Your Grace is too formal for the affection we share for one another, and I have no liking for the word stepmother."

Evanna called to mind a young lady boarder who had stayed with her, an emigree from the continent. "Madre?"

Cairstine squeezed her hand. "Yes, I like it. A special word for us to use between ourselves."

The subject of mother and child being on both their lips, it did not seem untoward for Evanna to ask. "How did you know about James? When your belly swelled?"

"Good gracious, no." Cairstine smiled. "I couldn't have waited that long. I suspected, of course, but the local midwife confirmed it."

Evanna would have liked to ask more, but they had reached the foot of the stairs, so held her peace.

Chapter Ten

Nathan took his chance to summon Sydney while the ladies were out of the room and sent him on his errand to the Assembly Rooms. Duncan's eyebrows raised a little when he gave his final instruction to the lad. "Return the answer directly to me. No one else."

He explained when he and Duncan were once more alone. "Evanna is taking Cairstine shopping this afternoon while you and I call at the Assembly Rooms. However, if I receive the information I seek, we shall be paying a private call on Lady Kerr instead. We encountered her carriage on the road to Edinburgh. I suspect she's here in an attempt to wheedle or coerce her way back into daughter's life now she's about to become a duchess, and I will not allow it."

Duncan frowned. "Would she dare? Having cast her daughter off so thoroughly."

Nathan had been happy to confide some of the history behind his and Evanna's relationship to Duncan and Cairstine, although none of the finer detail. "I must admit I put the notice of the wedding in the *Scottish Times* to thumb my nose at the Kerrs, so to speak, but that Lady Kerr has had the gall to turn up in the city at this time is an unwelcome surprise. Still, money was ever the Kerrs' driving force, so I can only think she has come up with some kind of ploy to manipulate Evanna's emotions to her own financial advantage."

"And you will inform her it will not wash?" Duncan smiled.

"In no uncertain terms," Nathan stated grimly.

The door opened to readmit the ladies. Cairstine looked pointedly at the absence of a glass on the side-table, then at Duncan. He laughed and jumped to his feet. "Coming right up, my love."

Evanna sipped from her glass when it was brought to her. "Are you hungry? Shall I ring for food to be served?"

Cairstine shook her head. "We knew we would probably miss luncheon, Mrs P. I had the inn at Linlithgow pack up a basket of savoury pastries for us to eat on the coach. Do you have any plans for us this afternoon?"

"I'd value your opinion in selecting my wedding bonnet."

"And I would be honoured to do so." Cairstine smiled.

"I'll order the coach to be readied then, shall I?" Nathan enquired, trying not to sound too eager to be free to get on with his own plans.

Duncan jumped to his feet. "His Grace and I will take our carriage to the Assembly Rooms. I'll tell Robbie to harness fresh horses."

Cairstine looked first at him then her husband. "Hmmm... You two are up to something..."

His daughter was as sharp-eyed as ever. Nathan tried to relax casually back against his chair. "No, no. Just eager to taste the wines."

"Hmmm…"

She made no more objection though and threaded her arm through Evanna's when the carriage was announced. Duncan followed them into the hall to wave them farewell and, as if he'd been waiting for the coast to be clear, Sydney popped his head around the door. "She's there, yer Grace. Number twelve Chamber Street, just off the Royal Mile."

"Well done, laddie. Go to the kitchen and tell Cook I said she's to give you an iced bun."

Sydney didn't need telling twice and with a huge grin sped off.

Duncan reappeared. "You have the address?"

Nathan nodded, and they walked outside to the street where Robbie, in the Callander equipage, was waiting. It took less than ten minutes for him to tool them to the residence of Mrs Mhairi McPherson and, once they alighted, Nathan rapped the head of his cane on the front door. A footman opened it and offered a silver tray for an introductory card.

"No," Duncan barked peremptorily. "The Duke of Glenard and the Earl of Callander do not proffer cards and wait for admittance. You will conduct His Grace into Mrs McPherson's presence immediately and announce our names at the door."

The footman goggled at them. High-ranking peers obviously did not come to the house very often. "Yes, Your Grace. Of course, my lord. The ladies are gathered in the parlour. This way, this way…"

Nathan exchanged a glance with Duncan as the man bowed and scraped. Neither of them treated their servants in such a high-handed manner, but it was necessary this time if their entrance was to have the desired effect. The footman stopped in front of a wooden door and raised his arm to knock. Nathan stayed him with the head of his cane. "Just open it and announce us, good and loud."

The servant swallowed hard and did as he was bid. Nathan swept past him with Duncan one step behind him. Three ladies, each displaying various looks of surprise, stared. Bony, and far more angular than he remembered, Lady Kerr was one of them. Nathan's bile rose at the sight of her. He looked down his nose at each of the women in turn, until they remembered their manners, rose to their feet and dipped him the low curtsey due to his ducal rank. Mrs McPherson was the first to recover.

"I am honoured, Your Grace, by your visiting my humble house."

"You won't be. Sit."

Mrs McPherson's mouth dropped open as they retook their seats. "I…I…don't understand your meaning, Your Grace."

The remembrance of Evanna's injuries stiffened his resolve. "You, madam, must have known the manner of the man your brother was. In kindness, I will presume that during your childhood, for your own preservation, you learnt not to confront him. But as a grown woman that does not excuse you. You did not warn your friend. By your silence, you allowed the violence he inflicted on her daughter…"

Mrs McPherson's cheeks reddened, and she turned her face away.

"Violence… What violence?" Lady Kerr spluttered.

Nathan turned his gaze on her. "And you in your avarice, madam, made no proper enquiry as to the qualities of the man. You sold your daughter for the shekels Percival-Smyth offered, and when he cast her off as unworthy, you accepted his judgement and didn't so much as contact her."

"Mr Percival-Smyth came and told us all. Evanna was stubborn. Disagreeable. Defiant. By his generosity he agreed to make no public comment, and although she was unfit to live with him in the same house as his wife, he provided her with accommodation and income for the rest of his life."

Nathan's anger boiled through his veins. Was the woman really so obtuse? "And why did you accept his word without question? Because he assured you he would not renege on the financial promises he had made you?"

"Mr Percival-Smyth was a man of honour," Lady Kerr said stubbornly.

In icy tones of cold rage, Nathan hissed, "He was not, and Evanna still bears the scars. An honourable man does not bind a woman's hands and whip her mercilessly to within an inch of her life for any reason whatsoever."

The younger of the three women began to cry and covered her mouth with her hands. From a passing resemblance to Evanna, Nathan guessed she was Robina and turned to her. "If you, Miss Kerr, ever find yourself in danger of being similarly sold down the river, you may apply to me for assistance, and it will be forthcoming…" He turned back to face the two older women. "But as for you two, stay away from Evanna. Do not doubt my influence in this matter. If I catch sight of either of your faces again, I will shred your reputations so low not even the lowest gutter rat will acknowledge your existence."

He turned on his heel, and Duncan grim-faced beside him commented as they stalked out of the room. "I didn't know it."

"Evanna would prefer it if that continued be the case. It's not a period of her life she cares to recall, or has any need to, now the bastard is planted six feet underground."

* * * *

Evanna took a swatch of material with her to the milliner's. Cairstine compared it to the silk flowers on offer and selected roses of pearlised blue. "Nearly a perfect match. I don't think you'll find better."

Evanna agreed then tried on several bonnets. One with a poke brim was deemed most flattering, on which the milliner would attach the flowers that matched the colour of her wedding dress. They returned to Acheson House, and Cairstine ran up to the nursery to spend an hour with her son while Evanna sought the solace of an hour asleep on the bed in her own room. Janet woke her as the clock struck five and Evanna yawned then contemplated her maid. She was not as young as Maisie had been, so could possibly possess the knowledge Evanna had not been able to ask Cairstine. She took a breath in then asked as casually as she could, "Ah...you have brothers and sisters, do you, Janet?"

"Aye, I mean yes, ma'am." Janet bobbed. "Eight of 'em. An' I'm the eldest."

"Goodness. Your mother has kept the midwife busy."

"Ol' goodwife McNally hae seen us all into the world, like she's done wi' most of the bairns around our way. No one better Ma says."

"Having never produced a child, I unfortunately lack knowledge of how a pregnancy proceeds, or of the manner in which a child is birthed, and yet, come Saturday, the welfare of the many families living on the duke's estate will become my responsibility. An hour of goodwife McNally's time could go some way to rectifying the matter for me. Oblige her to call on me tomorrow morning, please?"

"Of course, ma'am."

A monetary reward would ensure Mrs McNally's attendance, so Evanna took a golden coin from her purse and laid it on the mantle. "A guinea will be waiting for her trouble."

More money than a midwife could ever hope to earn in over half a year. Janet's eyes widened at the size of the largess on offer. Evanna dipped her fingers back into her purse and placed a silver crown beside it. "For yourself. Bring her to visit me quietly. This is no one's business but my own."

Janet gawped at the mantle open-mouthed. "For me? To keep? Nae gae ta ma maw?"

Her reaction told Evanna she had guessed correctly — like most housemaids, Janet's wages were sent home to support the myriad of children in her family. "To spend as you wish."

"Oh, thank you, ma'am." Janet said fervently. "I'll bring her ta ye by way of thon back stairs, I promise."

Her maid assisted her to dress for the evening and dinner proved a languorous affair. Fine wines and good food after an activity-filled day left none of them inclined to stay up late and burn the midnight oil.

Evanna made her way up to bed shortly after ten, and once in the privacy of her room, stripped naked and replaced her dress with a silken robe. Then she set the window ajar and lay down on the bed. Tinkling notes of a pianoforte floated through the window along with the soft hum of conversation she remembered so well. The bedroom door opened, and Nathan slipped into the room. She patted the bed, and he kicked off his shoes and joined her. "Can you hear it?" she smiled. "I used lie here night after night wondering who could hold so many parties. It is such a happy sound."

Nathan chuckled and took her into his arms. "And then you discovered the nature of the parties."

"To my delight," she assured him.

They lay entwined. Evanna snuggled closer to listen to the good-natured revelry...and opened her eyes however much later. Oh, no! She'd fallen asleep. "Nathan, I'm sorry. I didn't mean to."

He kissed into her hair. "I'm not surprised you're tired out, my love. You've had a lot to do this past week or so. Let's stay in bed. The Temple can wait. There'll be other nights. Lots of them."

"I would like to be up to snuff to enjoy our wedding day," she admitted.

"That's settled then. Get under the covers and I'll tuck you in."

Evanna removed her robe and slipped beneath the sheets while Nathan divested himself of his clothes, lay beside her and pulled the coverlet up. The pillow soft beneath her cheek, she sighed happily as Nathan pressed his body against her back. She enjoyed his warmth, his closeness. He put his arm over her waist, and she smiled knowing what his hand would seek. Nathan adored her large, generously plump breasts as much as she loved his touch — gentle, reverent, never rough.

She wiggled her buttocks against his groin as he stroked and felt his shaft harden.

"You want me, my love?"

Wet at the very thought of him inside her, Evanna lifted her rear. "Always."

He moved his fingers to the throbbing place in between her legs, teased her open and inserted his cock. She sighed as he filled her and rocked her hips. He held her to him and pushed forward in time with her movement. Slow, intense, he thrust, the sensation building until she mewled at the waves of pleasure pulsating through her pelvis. Nathan groaned as his climax arrived, and still entwined, they lay curled together until sleep arrived.

* * * *

Evanna stirred again when Nathan kissed her shoulder. "I'll slip back to my bedroom. Sleep on, my love."

Nothing loath, Evanna drifted off once more and woke again when Janet brought her morning hot chocolate into the room. Normally, Evanna replaced her nightgown after making love, but she was still naked so left the coverlet pulled up to her chin. "Set it down, please. I shall not require breakfast this morning. Bring Mrs McNally to me when she arrives."

"I'll whisk her up the back stairs, ma'am. Nae a body will realise who she's here to see."

Evanna dismissed her maid then performed her morning ablutions and dressed with shaking hands. The door re-opened a few minutes after the mantle clock struck nine, and Janet escorted into the room a woman who to all appearances was some years younger than Evanna had expected. In her mind's eye, midwives dressed in black and were of the elderly, wise-old-woman, persuasion. This one was younger than she was herself and was wearing a navy-blue gown of worsted — practical and of good quality.

"Good morning, ma'am. You have need of my services, I hear?" Her voice was low and melodious. Evanna guessed it would be soothing and encouraging for anyone in labour to hear.

Evanna nodded at Janet to leave them. "Please take a seat."

Mrs McNally sat and Evanna took the chair opposite her.

"I've worked alongside my mother since I was twelve, in case you were a-wondering, madam. Running and fetching at first, then helping properly as she taught me the lore of childbirth. Forty years and more she brought bairns into this world, but Mother is largely retired now for the arthritis that has twisted her hands. My title of Mrs is honorary. My calling is to continue her work, not birth bairns of my own."

Reassured the midwife, despite her lack of years, knew her stuff, Evanna ventured a question. "Forgive my ignorance, but I know little of the actualities of the subject and I wish to. To my understanding, a woman conceives a child, and her monthly courses cease for the nine months it takes for the babe to grow inside her, then there is the labour of delivery and it is born, but when does a mother actually know she is with child? Does she have to wait until her belly swells?"

The midwife wasn't fooled for a minute and guessed the question was being asked on Evanna's own behalf.

She looked into her eyes with an understanding smile. "How many courses have you missed?"

"Four, and nearing five," Evanna admitted.

"Lay on the bed. I shall have to pull up your skirt."

Steeling herself, Evanna did as she was bid. Would the method be intimately intrusive?

It was not. Goodwife McNally pushed up her skirt and lowered her drawers, but only to the base of Evanna's hips. She pressed Evanna's lower belly with the flat of her hand, then the side of it, before moving upward a tiny bit and pressing again.

"Hmmm…yes…a small bulge, but definitely a bulge. There is a babe in your belly, for sure."

Evanna let out a breath she didn't realise she'd been holding. "It's true? I'm with child?"

The midwife nodded sagely. "No mistaking it. You're rounded inside. Not enough to show outside your belly, but enough for me to feel a babe is in there."

Evanna sat up and rearranged her skirts, delighted wonderment flooding through her. She laughed out loud. She couldn't help it. "How wonderful. His Grace will be delighted, as am I."

"A happiness for you both." Mrs McNally smiled.

Evanna put her feet to the floor and took another guinea from her pocket. "Your discretion for the next few days would be much appreciated."

"You would have it anyway, but I'll not say no. Recompense for services I render often comes in the form of food and such jobs as I need doing on my cottage. Any coins I receive are put away for the time when my old age, like Mother's, denies my offering my skills."

Evanna didn't hesitate to share her joy. "When this child is born, every year on the anniversary of its birth, you shall receive another." Mrs McNally smiled and with her blessings departed.

Evanna took a deep breath as she left the room. When to share the news with Nathan? She was bursting to tell him, but wanted them to be alone, and the house was about to get busier with the arrival of George and Grace. An idea occurred. After the ceremony. It was the most perfect wedding gift she could give her new husband — at least she hoped he would find it so.

* * * *

Nathan did not hold himself surprised when Evanna was not at breakfast. He'd shaken the dust of Corbridge from his heels leaving a rented house he'd lived in for less than two years, while she'd packed and said goodbye to the life she'd lived for over twenty. When she entered the parlour she appeared full of grig though.

The Armstrongs had recently arrived. George was sat on the chaise with Georgina on his lap and his wife Grace beside him, while Cairstine, Duncan and himself were ranged around them in varying armchairs. George made to rise and Evanna waved him down. "No need to stand on ceremony for me. Don't disturb yourself." She walked closer, kissed his cheek then knelt down and cooed as she stroked the baby's cheek. "Well, don't you look like your papa?"

Her words echoed Nathan's thoughts, and he was sure those of Cairstine and Duncan, although none of them had said so out loud. The resemblance between George and his *adopted* daughter was really rather obvious. Her blue, blue eyes in shape and colour, along with the little cleft in her chin, were mirror images of his own.

Cairstine snorted. "Mrs P!"

George didn't bat an eyelid. "Yes, there's really no mistaking it."

The cat now out of the bag, the atmosphere in the room relaxed. Evanna greeted Grace with a brief hug. "I've been longing to meet the lady who captured dear George's heart."

Nathan smiled. Evanna's down-to-earth sociability set everyone at ease. The conversation became more general and by the end of the day Grace had firmly been admitted into the inner circle of their close family and friends.

* * * *

One more night was Nathan's last thought as he prepared for bed. On the morrow he would once more be a husband. The house being so full of guests, and the wedding ceremony being early at eleven, he was spending this last night alone in his room, as was Evanna.

The morning dawned bright and clear with only a small breeze that in no way would disturb the ladies' bonnets. Nathan dressed with precision and care, his wedding suit including a certain natty waistcoat, striped in green and grey, re-made by Evanna's request—a replica of the one she had admired on the evening they had first met at the Assembly Rooms.

He walked to the kirk with Duncan and George, leaving the carriages for the use of the ladies, and waited in the sunshine for Evanna's arrival at the door. The ducal coach pulled up promptly at five minutes to the hour. Sydney jumped down from the box, opened the door and Evanna stepped out—beautiful in silken blue, the roses on her bonnet matching the colour of her gown. He walked to her and offered her his arm. "Shall we?"

She stretched up to kiss his cheek then threaded her arm through his. "Let's."

The kirk was full as they sauntered up the aisle as casually as if they were taking a walk around the park. He noticed Evanna's eyes searching the congregation. Guests had been invited but still the kirk was a public place. She could well be anxious her mother might turn up, so he squeezed her hand and reassured her. "She will not be here. I've cooked her goose, good and proper."

Evanna's glanced sideways at him and her dimple appeared. "You know me so well. Thank you."

The minster waited for them, his prayer book open. They repeated their vows and after Nathan slipped his ring on her finger then signed the register. In less than twenty minutes the deed was done. The smiles of their well-wishers followed them back down the aisle then they climbed into the coach that would take them to the Assembly Rooms for the real celebration to begin.

Nathan grinned as Sydney jumped onto the box alongside the coachman. "At least our nuptials evinced no cheeky remarks from him today to put you to the blush."

Evanna took his hand and laid it on her stomach. "Had he done so he would not have been wrong."

He looked into her eyes and saw her soft smile. *A baby!*

"I am to be a father again…?"

"Our babe will be with us a few weeks before Christmas. Will you mind?"

The joy of it being so burst forth. He pulled her close and kissed her soundly.

"My dearest love, you have just made me the happiest man alive, twice in one day!"

Want to see more from Cassie O'Brien? Here's a taster for you to enjoy!

From a Lady to a Maid
Cassie O'Brien

Excerpt

"Amelia. Amelia Brown. Where are you?"

I pulled my hands from the chill depths of the stone sink and wiped their numbness on the front of my pinny as I walked around the corner of the scullery into the kitchen and halted in front of the tall, bony figure of Ashton Manor's housekeeper.

"I'm here, Mrs. Price."

Mrs. Price peered at me over the top of half-glasses perched on her beak of a nose and sniffed. "Are the saucepans from lunch clean? The china from afternoon tea?"

The material of my dress cut into my armpit as I breathed in to speak. I pulled on the side seam of my bodice and eased the fabric away from my chafed skin. "Yes, Mrs. Price. I've just finished."

My movement provided some relief under my arm but tightened the material around my waist and I wriggled. Mrs. Price frowned.

"Amelia, kindly stand still when I'm talking to you. Why are you so pink in the face?"

I pulled on the front of my dress and shift to try to find a little room inside, so my chest could expand. "My clothes are too tight."

Mrs. Price looked at the stretched stitches on the side seam of my dress. "Are your laces tied at the end of their length?"

I nodded. "Yes, Mrs. Price. I can loosen them no farther."

"Yes, well…I believe it's your name-day?"

"Yes, Mrs. Price. I turned nineteen today."

"Are you sure? I wouldn't have put you at more than fourteen when I took you on as a tweenie maid last year." Mrs. Price's gaze moved down to my toes then back to my head. "Still, even I can see you've grown quite considerably since then."

"Yes, I'm sure, Mrs. Price. The day of my birth is written in the bible at home. I've grown this last year, I'm afraid."

Mrs. Price sniffed. "You can read?"

"Yes, Mrs. Price. I've had some schooling."

"Yes, well…you may have a larger dress and shifts today, as it's your name-day. Come and see me before supper. Now tidy that hair back under your cap and go and find Ellen to attend to the fires Above Stairs."

I wound a strand of my hair around my finger and tucked it under my cap. Mrs. Price walked away, her black dress rustling, and I let myself out of the kitchen door into the back yard. Cold February air wrapped itself around my body and I shivered as I trotted through damp mizzle to the sound of clunks on metal toward the glow of the oil lamp sitting on the ground by the coal shed. Ellen shoveled a last scoop into the second of two coal scuttles as I arrived.

"Ellen, you've filled mine for me. I thank you."

Ellen smiled as she put the shovel inside the coal shed and latched its door. "Well, as it's your birthday…"

I tugged on my dress and sucked in what air I could. "Mrs. Price says I may have another dress and shifts tonight. I can't wait. I can hardly breathe."

"I know. One set a year isn't enough, is it? You do know you've got to give the ones you're wearing back to Mrs. Price for the next maid who would fit them?"

"She'll be welcome to them." I winced. I gripped my scuttle handle with both hands. "Ready?"

Ellen nodded, turned down the wick of the lamp and grasped hers. I tensed my arm muscles, heaved my scuttle upward and followed her through the back yard toward the yellow glow of the oil lamp sitting on the kitchen window sill. Mrs. Price, sitting at the long, wooden table I scrubbed daily, looked up from counting a pile of linen napkins in front of her as we staggered in.

"Plenty of time before the dressing gong," she said. "Make sure you're finished and back Below Stairs when you hear it."

I followed Ellen to the green, baize-covered door that led to the flights of wooden servants' stairs that allowed us access to the upper floors of the Family's living quarters of Ashton Manor. Six flights later, I stood beside her, puffed and rested my scuttle. Ellen pushed open the green swing-hinge door that separated the realm of servant from that of Family and peeked around it.

"No sign of any of them," she said over her shoulder.

I hefted my scuttle and stepped around her onto the softness of red carpet, walked with her into a hallway of closed, polished wooden doors illuminated by whiter light from the cleaner burn of paraffin lamps suspended by chains overhead and my dress pinched me again.

"Thank the Lord. It's quicker when they're not in their bedrooms, and I could do with quick tonight," I puffed out.

Ellen stopped walking and looked me. "Your face is awfully pink. You stop here on the Bachelors' wing and just do His Lordship's. I'll run down and do the three Ladies'."

"Ellen, that's kind of you. I'll do your potty duty tomorrow morning. I'll be well by then, once I can catch my breath again."

Ellen grinned. "Fires in exchange for chamber pots? I'll take that trade anytime, I thank you. I'll meet you behind the green door on the half-landing when we've finished."

Ellen walked up the hallway toward the Ladies' bedrooms. I tapped on His Lordship's door, received no answer and opened it to find the side lamps lit, as well as the ceiling fitting. I left the door open behind me as I walked in, a signal to the room's occupant that a servant — other than his valet, Mr. Hubert — was in his room, should he return to it.

The pain shot through my ribcage as I put my scuttle down, knelt before the fire and stretched forward to rake the hot coals with the poker. My ears filled with a soft buzz and the flicker of the flames hazed before my eyes. I sat back on my heels and breathed in as deep my dress would allow when it dawned on me how close I had come to passing out face-down into the fire.

I looked over my shoulder and heard only silence from the hallway, so reached into the scooped neckline of my dress and unfastened the first few buttons of my modesty shift. My breasts billowed upward into a décolleté normally only seen on the Ladies of the house when dressed for a ball, but the cramp in my ribs eased and my vision settled. I bent forward and re-applied the poker, listening for the sound of a footstep or the dressing gong, glanced backward to pull the scuttle closer and saw a pair of male legs encased in buckskin riding breeches and soft-soled leather boots walk into the room.

I pinched my shift together as best I could with one hand, kept my back turned and carried on working the poker with the other, as if I hadn't seen a Lord enter the room, while I tried to think of a way to get my breasts decently covered again without my doing so being noticed.

"Will you be much longer?" he asked.

"My apologies, My Lord. I didn't hear the dressing gong."

"It hasn't been rung yet. I'm early."

The whisper of leather footwear on the move warned me I had no time to consider any discreet option. I weighed the idea of making a dash for the door, looked down at my chest and realized even more breast would be exposed if I jumped up to run, so decided that if I was to be discovered with more than an appropriate amount of flesh on display, it was not going to be while I was on the floor kneeling at anyone's feet.

I hung the poker alongside the other fire irons, stood and tipped the scuttle toward the flames then reached for my buttons and looked sideways at the boy, grown into a man, that I hadn't been this close to since I was seven years old. I saw no hint of recognition in his eyes, although they widened slightly as his gaze dropped to my open frontage. I recalled his attention to my face.

"If you wouldn't mind averting your eyes, My Lord."

A gleam of amusement lightened the blue of Damion's irises as he raised his gaze from my chest.

"I'd rather not. I believe I'm enjoying the view."

My heart thumped. I squared my shoulders as the servant in me sensed the offer of a quick tumble coming my way, and the woman I had been a year ago stiffened her spine and turned the offer aside in the manner I would have done then.

"Hardly befitting conduct, Sir. But as the fault is mine, enjoy away."

I put my hand on my breasts, pushed them inside my shift, refastened my buttons and picked up my scuttle.

Damion smiled. "It might have been more enjoyable if you'd permitted me to do that for you."

I didn't lower my gaze as I dipped my curtsey. "I thank you for your kind offer, Sir, but I believe I must decline. I do have a prior evening engagement that will amuse me more."

"With…?"

I stepped around him. "With the pans in the scullery that have just been used to provide your dinner."

I walked out of the room and Damion's soft laughter followed me, along with the hope that the sound of it meant the boy I had known had retained his sense of humor and Mrs. Price wouldn't be calling me to her room shortly to tell me to pack my box because of my cheek. She looked at me as I entered the kitchen.

"Ah, Amelia. Relieve yourself of your scuttle and come with me."

I put my scuttle outside the kitchen door, took a short breath in and followed her along the length of the drafty corridor to her sitting room. She walked over to a large cupboard and I let my breath escape as she opened the door to shelves of folded clothing.

"Try the dresses against yourself. Find one of better fit with enough give in the laces for farther expansion."

Mrs. Price reached in and shook creases from folded dresses and I held them against me until we found one that seemed roomy enough, along with two white cotton modesty shifts to wear beneath it.

"Let me have your old clothes back tomorrow."

"I thank you, Mrs. Price. I will."

Mrs. Price peered at me over the top of her glasses. "I didn't realize your age until you said it this morning, Amelia. It's not fitting that you're still a tweenie maid at nineteen. I have two positions vacant at the moment—laundry maid or under parlor maid. You've worked hard this year, so I will let you choose."

It took me no longer than ten seconds to make up my mind. A parlor maid's work was comprised of lighter duties than those in the laundry, but laundry maids worked mainly Below Stairs and out of the way of any visitors or house guests to Ashton Manor who might have seen me in more recent times than Damion and his family and would still recognize my face.

"I'd like the position of laundry maid, please."

Mrs. Price's eyes widened. "You're sure?"

"Yes. I thank you. It's the soap. I like to have clean hands."

Mrs. Price sniffed. "Well, if you're sure, pack your box and move out of the tweenies' bedroom and in with Molly. You may have one half-day a week to yourself without duties and an extra two guineas a year."

My heart lifted at the unexpected offer of extra salary, and I smiled. "I thank you, Mrs. Price. I like Molly. She was kind to me when I first came here, and two more guineas will be welcome."

Mrs. Price returned my smile. "You're a good girl, despite your tendency to laugh at odd moments, Amelia. Now run along. Staff supper will be served shortly."

I left Mrs. Price, ran to the kitchen, pressed my back against the wall for James and Bert to pass me with their hands full of jellies, blancmanges and a display of crystallized fruits to take Above Stairs for the Family's final remove and resigned myself to a last meal of pinched discomfort as the kitchen table filled for staff supper and dinner service came to an end for the Family. I sat beside Molly and pushed my bundle of new clothes under my chair.

"I can move into your bedroom with you tonight, Molly. I'm your new laundry maid."

Molly grinned at me, her smile wide but gappy from a missing eye-tooth she'd had to have pulled three months before.

"Well done, Amelia. Happy birthday. Shall I help you move your things after supper?"

"Yes, please, and my thanks, Molly. It will be lovely to share a bedroom with just you instead of being in with three others."

Mrs. Oates watched the table fill as James, Bert and Mr. Bennett returned from serving the dessert course Above Stairs, pulled a heavy copper pan from the warming oven, brought it to the table and released the savory smell of rabbit stew when she took the lid off and placed it before Mrs. Price for her to serve.

Mrs. Price sat at one end of the table, Mr. Bennett at the other, and I closed my eyes as he stood and intoned Grace. Mrs. Price ladled stew into thick pottery bowls and I dipped my spoon into one of the three hot meals a day that I now received, rather than the one sketchy offering daily that had been all my stepfather had allowed me before I'd left home and found my position at Ashton Manor.

The bell marked 'dining room' rang on the servants' board on the wall as we finished eating. Mr. Bennett stood, along with James and Bert, and they left the kitchen to clear the table and serve brandy to the men while Mrs. Oates poured boiling water into the lidded jug standing on a silver salver for the Ladies to make their tea. I looked at Mrs. Price.

"Mrs. Price, may Molly and I be excused so I may move my possessions into my new bedroom, please?"

She sniffed and inclined her head. "You may, but make sure you say the goodnight prayer yourselves if you are not to be present when Mr. Bennett says it here."

"Yes, Mrs. Price, we will," Molly and I chorused.

I let the green door swing shut behind us and Molly giggled as we ran up flights of wooden stairs. "I don't know about you, but it's not Mr. Bennett that's going to be in my prayers tonight. A kiss from James or Harry... That's what I'll be down on my knees and asking the heavens for."

I laughed and side-swiped her arm. "Molly! What about poor Fred? You were kissing him behind the stables last week."

Molly grinned. "And I'm going to kiss a few more, too, before I make up my mind who to walk out with."

About the Authors

Raven McAllan

After 30 plus years in Scotland, Raven now lives near the east Yorkshire coast, with her long-suffering husband, who is used to rescuing the dinner, when she gets immersed in her writing, keeping her coffee pot warm and making sure the wine is chilled.

With a new home to decorate and a garden to plan, she's never short of things to do, but writing is always at the top of her list.

Her other hobbies include walking along the coast and spotting the wildlife, reading, researching, cros stitch and trying not to drop stitches as she endeavours to knit.

Being left-handed, and knitting right-handed, that's not always easy.

Cassie O'Brien

I love:
Being with family and friends.
Writing and having the freedom to do so now child four of four has passed her driving test and is off to uni later this year.

I Like:
Any excuse to throw a party.
Any excuse to open a bottle of fizz.
Shoes in vast quantities – the higher the heel the better.

Ambitions:
To write many more books.
To own a pair of Louboutin's.
To never go near an iron or a hoover again.

Raven and Cassie love to hear from readers. You can find their contact information, website details and author profile page at https://www.totallybound.com

Home of Erotic Romance

Sign up for our newsletter and find out about all our
romance book releases, eBook sales and promotions,
sneak peeks and FREE romance books!